THE SCHLIMAZEL OF SEBREIM

RICHARD ELFMAN

Encyclopocalypse Publications
www.encyclopocalypse.com

PROLOGUE

Long ago, in the Transcarpathian Mountains, that remote region where the Ukraine borders Romania and Hungary, lay a dirty little village named Sebreim. It is a wonder why anyone of importance might have given even a thought to such an insignificant, far away place. Yet none-the-less, the mighty Hapsburgs to the West, and Catherine the Great to the East, quarreled endlessly over every inch of their potential empires. Including dirty little Sebreim. Diplomats and emissaries did their best. Was war the only option? So in order to prevent things from boiling over, it was agreed upon that *something* must be found that everyone could agree upon. Evict the Jews, someone suggested. Brilliant! Diplomacy having prevailed once again, war between the Austro-Hungarian Empire and Imperial Russia was postponed until a later date.

The coarse and vulgar peasants of Sebreim were only too happy to comply with the order—and steal the houses and lands of their former neighbors of the past three centuries. All except the old Jewish washerwoman, Yachne, who, along with her two unfortunate sons Schlemihl and Schlimazel, was forced to stay and continue laboring over the town's laundry, as well as their ancient and diminutive assistant Genghis. Purportedly the sole remaining descendant of some other earlier invasion.

And life continued in Sebreim. And winter came as it always does, forcing the coarse and vulgar peasants to spend less time in the fields and more hours in the tavern. And Yachne was having trouble as usual, gagging from too much smoke under her boiling kettles.

———

Schlemihl is sent upon the roof to adjust the chimney flu he had *fixed* a hundred times. And true to his name, he slips, demolishing the chimney in the process and slides down the roof with a pile of stones. Fortunately, his fall is broken by his brother Schlimazel, who, true to his name, was approaching unaware with a pile of wood he had gathered from the forest.

Schlimazel is lucky that day. For only his nose is bloodied. His neck seems fine! Though that doesn't stop the victim from taking a good smack at his clumsy sibling. A scuffle ensues until the tiny, wizened Gengis manages to break it up with a few rudimentary judo flips.

"How do you do that?" queries Schlimazel.

"*Gong-foo Shao Lin Wang!*" replies the beady eyed little man, who apparently never learned to speak the local Slavic dialect. Or Yiddish. Or English. Or any other language that anyone else in this story speaks, including the narrator.

Back at the laundry, Yachne slaps and berates her sons. "A curse upon both of you!" She spits upon them three times. Schlemihl is assigned a basket of disgustingly soiled chamber linen and Schlimazel, the *unlucky* one, is sent off to the tavern with a load of clean towels and cloths. For he is the one who must face the *goyim*[1]. The villagers.

---

1. Gentiles

CHAPTER 1
BEAUTY AND THE BEASTS

AT THE TAVERN, DRUNKEN, RED-FACED MEN QUAFF THEIR DARK ale and throw bread, and an occasional mutton bone, at Gypsy musicians who valiantly serenade for their supper.

"You godless Gypsies are almost as bad as the Jews!" shouts Ivan, as his friends applaud his keen wit and insight. And, of course, as if right on cue, in walks Schlimazel.

He is immediately pelted by bread and taunted mercilessly by a chorus of Jew haters. Flying bread is followed by spoons and cups, and before even more harmful missiles are employed, Ludmilla, the innkeeper's fetching and buxom young daughter, hustles the unfortunate Hebrew into the back and out of harm's way.

"Dirty Jew!" yell Ivan and his cohorts, chortling and guffawing as they tear at their mutton with rotten teeth and never-washed hands.

In a room off the kitchen, Shlimazel helps Ludmilla put the linens away. "What happened to your nose?" asks the fresh-faced maiden.

"It is nothing," responds the sad faced young man. "And

my neck is fine." She brings him a steaming bowl of soup and sets it upon a small table.

"Oh taste it! I have put mutton in your soup today!"

"Ummn!" says Schlimazel, savouring his meal.

"And potato dumplings!" she smiles.

As he spoons in his sustenance, Ludmilla checks that the doors are well closed and carefully retrieves a pencil and lesson book from under some shelves.

"Will you teach me today?" she implores.

"I suppose, for a short time. I must return to work soon."

The peasant women of Sebreim, and most of the men for that matter, will not learn to read until Comrade Lenin enforces his second Five Year Plan, several centuries later. And even then, the curriculum will be quite limited. But in the meantime, Schlimazel enjoys teaching his eager and curious pupil. For Ludmilla offers him more than just a warm bowl of soup, generously laden with chunks of mutton and delicious potato dumplings. She offers him the only kindness that he knows. A kindness he doesn't even get from his own family.

"The—rain—in the—Ukraine—falls mainly—on the —PLAIN!" cries Ludmilla, bursting with pride.

And that isn't all that is almost bursting—as Shlimazel avoids her swollen young bosoms trying the limits of her low-slung blouse, as well as his patience and willpower. And in Sebreim, that is a place where he dare not even think about! Oy vey! Oy vey! *Oy vey!* (And with his luck!)

Meanwhile, in the tavern, drunken muscular men do impressive dance maneuvers from down on their haunches. Even more impressive is when they leap in the air, fly across the room and bounce off the walls with flashing swords in mock battle, only occasionally slicing a cranium or severing a finger. These boys may be stupid as the potatoes that sustain them, but they are also the spawn of warriors such as Attila the Hun, Genghis Khan and even the mighty Vikings, who once pillaged their way down the Danube all the way to the Black Sea. Not to mention more recent generations of Cossack armies with their signature haunch launched dance steps so popular with the peasants of Sebreim .

And in the next room, our ill-fated hero bids his goodbye, hoping the drunken peasants don't bother him too much on the way out. Fat chance of that, he thinks.

Thankfully Ludmilla, in her wisdom and kindness, pulls Schlimazel by the *payyes*[1] and nudges him through the side window. He falls to the snow and hurts his nose a bit. But his neck is still fine! Schlimazel, vainly searches for the positive, while trying to clear his mind of Ludmilla's voice, the scent of her hair, the warm feel of her tender young bosom, pressing ever so lightly against his arm—Oy vey! Oy vey! *Oy vey!* He trudges through the snow, grumbling quietly to himself.

---

1. Long side curls worn by Jewish boys and young men

CHAPTER 2

WHAT THEY DON'T TEACH
YOU IN HEBREW SCHOOL

BACK HOME AT THE LITTLE LAUNDRY MILL, THE SHREWISH YACHNE berates Schlimazel. "What? I send you for a minute, you take an hour?"

He thinks fast and improvises a little. "The peasants held swords to my throat, forcing me to stand upon the table on one leg while holding full mugs of ale out in either hand!"

"Well—good that it was you. Your brother would surely have spilled one of them." She spits three times.

Schlemihl grins like an idiot from across the room, barely able to suppress his glee.

"You think that's funny?" barks Schlimazel.

"Shut up, both of you!" she snaps.

"But I didn't say anything!" protests the sibling.

Yachne takes her little pipe out and lights it. "We are leaving tomorrow night."

"Leaving?" they ask.

"Yes." A pin could drop. "For Bucharest."

"*Bucharest!?*"

"I have three official permits that your uncle the finagler

has sent us. We'll grab our things quietly, when the *goyim* are asleep, and be gone from this cesspool." She takes a puff from her pipe and spits three times.

"And what about Gengis?" queries Schlimazel.

"What—you want I should give him your permit?"

Schlimazel doesn't think that is fair. But he doesn't say anything either.

"Now go to sleep!" And Yachne goes off to her little room behind the laundry, joined by Genghis a short time later, who she has slept with for the past nineteen years; Ever since the week after her poor husband, Moishe, died—which is another story, so don't ask!

Schlemihl and Schlimazel settle into their little sleeping area, upon piles of dirty laundry. The room is frigid, as the fires have long been extinguished to save fuel.

"Bucharest!" exclaims Schlemihl. "What a marvelous place that will be! The ghetto there is said to have many young *yiddishe maidels.*[1]"

"Yes." says Schlimazel, half heartedly. Somehow, things never seem to work out for him. Only what will it be this time, he wonders? And soon enough, as his brother begins to snore loudly with sweet dreams of the Bucharest ghetto, comes a tapping at the window. It's Ludmilla! Oy! He scrambles over to her. Her eyes are red from tears. She is trying to tell him something. He signals her to shush and ushers her in through the front door.

"Please, can we talk?" she asks anxiously.

"Of course—just try and keep your voice down a second." He lights a candle and takes her to a private closet were they sit on a soft pile of laundry. Clean laundry.

"Oh, Schlimazel—this is the most terrible thing—the most terrible thing." And she begins to sob upon his shoulder.

"I'm sure it is very terrible." He tries to comfort her. "But what is it?"

"My father has agreed to marry me to Ivan!"

"Ivan? That ruffian! That cretin! That *schmendrik*[2]!?" Ludmilla begins to sob even harder, so that Schlimazel must hold her tight and try to quiet her down a bit. Finally, after no tears are left, she rests her weary head upon his chest.

"Oh, Ludmilla. This is terrible. And just when I am leaving."

"Leaving?"

"Yes. For Bucharest, tomorrow."

"But you cannot leave! You are the only one who understands me—that I aspire to more than the life of a cow, who breeds and *shleps*[3], as your people say, in this dirty, terrible village. Without a kindred soul to talk to—that is a fate even worse than Ivan." Not a simple thought for such a seemingly simple girl. She rests her cheek against his and sobs quietly.

They sit snuggled together, long after the candle has gone out. Finally, as the first rooster begins to crow, Ludmilla gives Schlimazel a gentle, tender kiss. Upon the lips. And with that, she slips away into the fading night. *Oy vey!* Schlimazel's head is spinning and his heart is light. This is the stuff they didn't teach him about in Hebrew school!

And creeping faster than the first rays of the rising sun, the approaching sound of Yachne's voice can be heard screaming his name. *"Schlimazel!"*

He rushes to laundry central, where Genghis is already stoking the fires and Schlemihl is loading clothes.

"Quick!" says Yachne. "We must get the laundry done by noon and quietly pack our things by sundown. Then we leave by the back, without a fuss."

They go about their work. Schlimazel is dismayed to see his mother, explain/mime, "charade" style, to Genghis, that she and the boys will be gone for a few days and that he should mind the laundry.

Schlemihl is excited as can be. Schlimazel has only a numb feeling. The day passes quickly. Schlimazel's only good luck is that the roughest of the peasants are gone when he makes his delivery to the tavern. Ludmilla is working with her father, Grigor, the innkeeper, and can only send Schlimazel a furtive glance as he passes. But that fleeting moment, when their eyes connect, may as well have the force of lightning. Regardless of the impossible odds, this is when Schlimazel decides that he is not leaving. At least not yet. His luck may not be the greatest, but if nothing else, God made him smarter than they are. That he much *knows*.

Back at the laundry, Schlimazel works up all his courage to confront Yachne. Finally—"I am not going!"

"Fine, we'll give your permit to Genghis."

"You would probably bring bad luck along the way," adds his brother.

"That is what I was thinking as well," says the mother.

Schlimazel is secretly hurt at how easily this went. Genghis saw that something was amiss and is very glad to be leaving. When Yachne is out back with some chores, Schlimazel manages to corner the little guy.

"*Gong-foo, Shao Lin Wang!*" Schlimazel strikes a fighting pose.

The old man throws him with a rudimentary Judo toss. Schlimazel makes Genghis teach him this move, and a few others as well, over and over, until Yachne interrupts with her usual cursing and spitting.

An hour later, the sun sets and a full moon rises. Snow has begun to fall. Yachne, Genghis and Schlemihl depart along the back road with a donkey carrying their things. The next village is maybe two hours away. Schlimazel watches them leave, again feeling more numb than sad. The bright orange moon looks large and surreal.

---

1. Jewish maidens
2. idiot
3. carries, or hauls things

CHAPTER 3
GONG FOO SHAO LIN SCHLIMAZEL

OVER AT THE TAVERN, IVAN AND HIS BAND STAGGER IN FROM THE fields, covered in mud, drunk and boisterous. They have been tending the cows and the sheep. But in a manner that the Bible clearly forbids! For Christianity came late to these parts and pagan habits stubbornly linger.

"Fetch us food!" shouts Ivan to Ludmilla. His friends roar with approval. She looks at them with disgust.

"Don't look sad, betrothed young maiden," says one of the farm jockeys, "for Ivan is the *best* among us and you shall not go wanting when under his masculine yoke. A cow and *two* sheep he has taken today!"

"And compared to that, a simple girl like you shall be easy!" boasts Ivan, to even greater laughter and approval. Besides being the town bully, he is also considered the town wit.

"You will have to kill me first!" shouts Ludmilla, who turns to leave. But her father, Grigor, catches her playfully, giving her an affectionate squeeze on the rear.

"She will give you a fight, my son, like any good virgin

should, but your conquest shall be the sweeter, just like her mother's was!"

Ludmilla spits in her father's eye and runs upstairs, just as Schlimazel enters with a small bundle of laundry that they certainly don't need at this hour. He has been lurking in the doorway and has seen too much. A foot deftly trips him and he falls gracelessly in on his laundry. A goblet of ale is spilled on his face. Peasants laugh and guffaw heartily. This is turning out to be the most fun of days for them!

———

Ludmilla is sprawled on her bed. She can tell by the level of jeering below that something major is going on below. Is that the voice of Schlimazel? She rushes back down to behold a piteous sight.

Schlimazel is on the table, standing upon one leg, arms outstretched with brimming goblets. Ivan holds a saber to his throat and forces him to perform and recite verses as the crowd convulses with laughter.

"I am a Jew. Hath not a Jew eyes? Hath a Jew not hands, organs, dimensions, senses, affections, passions?"

Ivan presses his sword even harder, for comic effect. *"If you prick us, do we not bleed? If you tickle us, do we not laugh?"*

The peasants are laughing so hard that tears stream down their faces. And *THWAP!* Ludmilla comes from behind and manages a deft kick between Ivan's legs which causes him to drop his saber, tipping Schlimazel in the process, who comes crashing to the floor in a pool of ale.

She grabs for the weapon. "Leave him alone, I *warn* you!"

Ivan easily disarms Ludmilla and shoves her away by the face.

"I shall teach you manners soon enough!" In Sebreim, as

elsewhere in the civilized world, a man cannot officially beat a woman *until* they are married. The crowd is wild with the sport at hand. Ludmilla has a complete fit and must be restrained by her hulking parents.

Schlimazel is given a bath of ale, until he manages to get up and strike his *gong-foo* pose. "And if you wrong us, shall we not *revenge*!?" And with that, Schlimazel flips Ivan! The room goes silent at the sheer audacity of this act.

"No, Schlimazel! Do not do this for me!" Ludmilla is in tears, afraid for her friend. Ivan gets up.

"Big man with the cows and the sheep, huh?" And Schlimazel tosses him again! Ivan rises in a state of extreme agitation. The crowd calls to him with encouragement. Schlimazel is bouncing around now like a Yiddish Bruce Lee. But when he goes to throw his oppressor once more, Ivan has figured out the move and does not budge. That is when the carnage begins. Ludmilla must be carried off and locked in her room as Ivan and his friends set upon her hapless hero.

Outside, a large, ominous moon illuminates the village as it is blanketed in snow. Noise of an ugly crowd emanates from the tavern, as it seems by the sound of it, that poor Schlimazel is being beaten within an inch of his life.

Finally, the door flies open and the Jew is thrown out, unconscious, into the freezing snow, perhaps for the elements to complete a job that only the sodden drunkenness of the villagers prevented them from doing themselves.

The snow is falling heavy and Schlimazel, laying almost face down, is soon covered in whiteness. He opens his eyes a crack, but cannot move. Is this the fate of Schlimazel? A faint smile plays upon his lips, as he always did manage a sense of humor, even when faced with this most extreme of circumstances—his frozen demise.

Images flash through his mind. Falling from the cradle as a

baby and landing on his head. His very first beating from a peasant. As a boy, ruining the clothes of the visiting Burgermeister. More beatings from stupid peasants. Accidentally dropping the holy Torah scrolls, which caused his expulsion from the yeshiva[1]. Oy, now that was a bad one! But although Schlimazel's life is passing before him, at least he has the satisfaction, however ironic, that he has finally stood up like a man and fought back!

As he awaits his fate, there comes the sound of approaching hooves. A team of sleek black horses with a regal black coach. And no driver! The carriage stops beside his prostrate form and the door opens. Sitting within is a beautiful lady. Like a vision or a painting, her skin is alabaster white, her lips of crimson. She beckons with a smile. Her motions are slow, surreal and inviting. Death is not so ugly, thinks Schlimazel. Then everything fades.

---

1. Jewish religious school for young men

CHAPTER 4
THE YIDDISH VAMPIRE

WHAT HAPPENS NEXT IS NOT SO CLEAR IN SCHLIMAZEL'S MIND. A montage of dreams and images. The blur of spinning carriage wheels. Howling wolves and winding mountain roads. The beautiful lady cradling a shivering Schlimazel like Madonna and yarmulked child. Her penetrating eyes and crimson smile, ever so beguiling. And then—her kiss. And another— upon his neck! And Pain. And Ecstasy! *Mostly* ecstasy, he thinks. And vivid swirls of colors, black and red. And deep feelings of Life and Death. And finally, the woman baring her soft white, ever so luscious, bosom. And with her fingernail, making a tiny mark upon the rosy nipple—drawing a drop of blood. And taking Schlimazel—to suckle him, like a baby. *Oy!* And did she say something about marriage?

Schlimazel doesn't remember, as he lies in the pre-dawn snow, somewhere high in the mountains. But instead of freezing with cold, he is feeling a little on the hot side. Odd? As a matter of fact, the approaching rays of the sun seem to fry him with heat! Fortunately, he has found himself at the mouth of a cave. He rushes in to take shelter from the—sun? *What?*

———

At the same moment, Ludmilla slides down from her attic window using a rope fashioned from bed sheets. She makes her way quickly to the little laundry building. The door is unlocked. No one is there. It is obvious the previous inhabitants had hurriedly packed and left. And with that, her heart breaks as she loses all hope.

Ludmilla returns home to a sound thrashing from her behemoth mother, Gorgoynia.

When that is finished, her father reads her the riot act. If Ludmilla fails to honor the marriage contract, according to law, Ivan's family will take title to the inn and Ivan shall marry the next in line: Ludmilla's plump little sister, Peytunya, a shy girl of twelve, which makes her legal in these parts of the Transcarpathian woods.

"Peytunia needs another year!" pleads Gorgoynia.

"Oh, she is ripe enough." bellows the father. "It's the inn we cannot afford to lose!"

"Don't worry." interjects Ludmilla, wishing she were dead. "I'll be his sow and you shall keep your inn—and Peytunya her maidenhead."

"Now that is the daughter I am proud of!" beams Grigor.

"I had the same worries before my wedding, also. But look at me now!" Gorgoynia smiles coyly with the single rotten tooth left in her mouth as Grigor affectionately kneads her ample buttocks.

———

Grigor thinks it wise to pay a visit to Ivan's family that day. Ivan's father, Ivanhoe'ya, is a gruff farmer, fat with profit from the expansion of his lands after the Jews were driven out.

"I have come to discuss the matter of our children, Squire Ivanhoe'ya."

"Yes?"

"I was wondering if would not be wise to advance the date of the marriage." Just then, Ivan wanders in from the fields, where he has been tending to his animals.

"What do you say, my son? Can you manage with your cows and sheep for two more months, until the arrival of spring, when you shall have the most ripe and beautiful young virgin in the village, hoping all the while that she does not change her mind?"

It is decided that Ivan has now had sufficient practice in the manly art of love, and in consideration of the bride's rampant emotionalism, caused by an overabundance of feminine juices in obvious need of release, that the wedding shall take place the coming Sunday. Ivanhoe'ya and Grigor toast with the farmer's best apple brandy: "To spirited women and horses—and their proper domestication!"

Sebreim is humming with talk of marriage preparations by the time the sun has set.

———

High in mountains, deep within a cavern, Schlimazel awakens once again. His mind seems clearer now. He tickles his palms and pinches his cheeks to determine that he *is*, in fact, still alive. But something is different. Something is *really strange*. He can see in the dark! This is odd. A bat flutters by. Faster than he can think, his hand darts like a bolt to snatch the beast from the air. Again, without thinking, he reflexively *bites its head off!* He looks in horror at what he has just done. My God! The taste of blood is on his lips. And he *likes* it!

High above the dirty little village of Sebreim, a plaintive

voice echoes from the lonely mountain cavern. "Oy vey! Oy vey! Oy vey! *Oy vey!*"

————

The week passes quickly in the village. Young maidens fuss about Ludmilla, all seething with hidden jealousy over her luck with the town's virile hero, son of a prosperous farmer. They pay her backhanded compliments and tell her the worst gossip. Ludmilla may as well be in a dream, as little seems real to her anymore.

Her younger sister, Peytunya, teases mercilessly, "Ivan shall split you like a Jewish bagel!"

"Shut your mouth! It is for *you* that I suffer, little wench!"

"*Nyah, nyah! Nyah, nyah!* A goose to be stuffed by sausage!"

"Ungrateful piglet!"

"It is *you* who shall squeal!"

"Shut your mouth, blabber-bucket of lard!"

"*Nyah, nyah! Nyah, nyah!*"

————

Meanwhile, high in the hills, after the sun has safely set, Schlimazel ventures out of his cave to scurry after small animals, or leap after them. At times, almost fly after them, bouncing off trees and up cliffs with incredible strength and agility. Schlimazel hasn't made sense of things yet, but in the meantime, he has to eat. Unfortunately, he must eat the blood of the living.

————

As the fateful Sunday approaches, Ivan's father drags him by the ear to confront a dead cow and a dead sheep. "You cannot restrain yourself two more days?"

"Did I do that? I will try and be more gentle next time."

The father shakes him violently. "You are getting married, numb skull! Save your juices for you bride!"

"Yes father, I will try."

Neither notices the small bloody puncture wounds on the animals' necks.

CHAPTER 5

CROUCHING TIGER, HIDDEN DRAYDL

Sunday comes with a cool, gray afternoon. In the village square, Ludmilla passes through the brief ceremony in a daze, like a sleepwalker. She wears the traditional country wedding dress, decorated with ancient weaving. Her hair is braided with flowers. As is Ivan's, per the local custom. The visiting priest is paid a few gold coins and hurries off to his next job in a nearby hamlet. And the peasants pile over one other to get to the free wedding feast.

The inn is soon packed with the entire adult population of Sebreim. Villagers gorge on massive chunks of pork and mutton, washed down by copious goblets of the strong local wine. Gypsy musicians play as peasants perform colorful folk dances and young men twirl and leap with their Cossack swords. Ivan and Ludmilla sit at opposite ends of an enormous banquet table, each now attired in a white linen nightgown, as is the custom, which they shall wear to their room for the consummation of their marriage.

Outside, night settles and a chill wind blows. But inside, drunken revelers are oblivious to all but the food in front of their faces. Ludmilla drinks more than her share, seeking an even deeper state of oblivion, for she would be happier going to her own funeral. Grigor stops chomping on his pork long enough to propose a toast.

"To my new son Ivan. May he bring wealth to our family, children to the village, and the same pleasure to my daughter —that all the cows and sheep can no longer enjoy!" Everyone applauds at Grigor's humor and well-turned phrase.

But not to be outdone in either wit or eloquence, Ivan stands proudly with his goblet raised. "May glory fall upon the land! May justice fall hard upon the Jews! And may no man or cow or sheep stand between me and my wife!"

People cheer and holler as the beaming groom drinks deeply from his marital cup. Until a well aimed kilo of mutton hits him square in the face, causing him to spill red wine over his fine white gown. Even the coarse and vulgar peasants of Sebreim find this very rude, although it does elicit a minor round of snickers.

"Who *dares* to throw meat in the face of my glorious son!?" demands, Ivanhoe'ya. A gust of wind whistles through the rafters, flickering the candles eerily and causing a pall to set upon the room. Then a voice answers from the shadows.

"Ivan is a pig with the mind of a dog—like the rest of you slavering cretins!" Angry guests spring up with swords. Who *dares* to insult them like this? "And that is even an insult to the pigs and the dogs!" he adds.

Enraged peasants look about for the impudent voice. And lo' and behold, seated in the dimness of a far back table, sits the Jew, Schlimazel, calmly spinning his *draydl*[1], yarmulke set to a rakish angle, cool as can be. Ludmilla smiles giddily, then faints.

Ivan is the first to leap upon the intruder, crying, "He is mine!" And Schlimazel promptly throws him with the exact same judo flip as before.

"So *dumb*, these goyim!" Ivan comes back and Schlimazel pretends to attempt the same move. Ivan smugly anticipates it and does not budge. But what he doesn't anticipate is the blur of raining blows and spinning kicks that carry him back across the room like a moving punching bag. *SMACK! PUNCH! KICK! PUNCH! SMACK!*

And when Schlimazel does his *Yiddishe* Bruce Lee bounce and cry this time, it seems a bit more appropriate. A man flies through the air with his saber. Schlimazel joins him mid-air with an elliptical, aerial roundhouse kick, avoiding the sword and demolishing the fellow's jaw in the process. More warriors leap at Schlimazel and all are dispatched with seeming ease and magical agility. At one point he even takes a seat to spin his draydl a little, while fighting off an entire row of attackers with his free hand. Ludmilla is taking this in with incredulous eyes. Not only is he a Superhero—but he can *read*!

Opponents are leaping off walls, twirling, slashing, punching and kicking, each with more gymnastic fighting ability than the last; only to be devastated by Schlimazel, whose grace and power can only be described as balletic. Except for the one moment when he jumps straight up in a corkscrewing ascent, only to hit his head upon a rafter, sending him crashing to the floor dazed, where a dozen ruffians quickly pile upon him. But a moment later Schlimazel springs in the air with a beautiful back flip and comes down kicking and fighting,

Yet still, the angry peasants continue on, without let up, crying, "Kill the Jew! Kill the Jew!" As they are unable to fathom that the boy whom they had so long pushed and spat upon was now rising up against them. Everyone, women as well as men, grab something sharp or hard as they set upon their former victim. Schlimazel pops across the room and lands on a table.

"*STOP!*" he says, with such intensity of purpose as to literally halt them in their tracks. Then, even more incredibly, the erstwhile bride rushes into his arms.

"Take me with you!" says Ludmilla. At this, the crowd is most aghast. It must be said that the diminutive and formerly reticent Schlimazel is pumped and glowing with charisma. With a grand dramatic flourish, he turns to the room, raises his arms like the bogeyman and for the first time, *bares his wicked fangs!* Men and women shriek in horror. All the fears and superstitions that these ignorant peasants harbor towards Jews has finally come to fruition and the citizens of Sebreim scramble for their lives, some jumping right through the windows.

Grigor and Gorgoynia scream to their daughter. "Run from the wicked demon! Run to Ivan, your husband!"

"*You* are all the wicked ones!" she shouts to the room, pressing closer to her hero, "And Ivan shall *never* be my husband!"

"But Ludmilla, something terrible has happened to me," Schlimazel indicates to his rather large incisors, "Can't you see?"

She glances at them but her decision has been made. "I declare myself your soul mate—and would go to hell and back with you!"

"Very well, because that is maybe where we are going." He gives her the type of major kiss that Clark Gable would later immortalize in Gone With the Wind. And off they go, semi-flying out the door.

Ivan comes staggering after them in his short, wine shmeared night shirt. "She is mine, filthy Jew! She is mine!" Ludmilla suddenly stops Schlimazel.

"Do you wish to turn back?" he graciously asks.

"No. But that *shmen-drik* must be warned not to touch my little pig-wench sister."

"Very well." Schlimazel fishes something from his pocket. "Then I shall hide the *draydl* where the sun does not shine." He drags Ivan back to the tavern, plucks a large candle and decorously slams the door. Ludmilla can hear Schlimazel singing over Ivan's cries. (In the style of Wayne Newton, though he hasn't been born yet:)

♪ *"O' draydl, draydl, draydl, I made it out of clay.*
And when it's dry and ready, O' draydl I shall play!" ♫

———————————

1. small spinning toy top with four sides

CHAPTER 6

BATMAN AND LUDMILLA

SCHLIMAZEL AND LUDMILLA ARRIVE AT THE CAVE WITH SMALL bundles of provisions hastily snatched from the village. They light a candle and venture inside. "Oy, Ludmilla! Is this not a cold, terrible place that I am taking you?"

"Compared to what you saved me from, this is the most wonderful place on Earth!"

They set up a little area for clothes, bedding, and some precious books that Schlimazel has brought. He gallantly makes his bed a little distance from hers.

"So I will be closer to the entrance," he explains, "to protect you from squirrels or bears." She acknowledges him coyly. Then after a while:

"Schlimazel?"

"Yes."

"Let me see those teeth again." He reluctantly lets her inspect his incisors. Although they seem smaller than in the tavern, they are definitely larger than normal human teeth.

"Schlimazel?"

"Yes."

"Do all Jews grow teeth like this? Maybe when the boys mature to men?"

"No, unfortunately. They give us a *bar mitzva*, completely harmless, that is all. The teeth is what happened after my —incident."

"Incident?"

And Schlimazel proceeds to tell Ludmilla the whole story, about the woman in the coach, the aversion to daylight, and after much reluctance, his unique dietary needs.

"She undressed herself like that and did this to you?"

"I was out of my mind, maybe I was dreaming."

"Oh, Schlimazel! Perhaps she was a witch and gave you a curse, or a disease. But do not worry. I will stand by you, until you are cured!" Ludmilla fights back tears. "I shall even stand by you if there is no cure!" But Schlimazel is determined to find a cure, now more than ever.

"Ironically, I have never felt so good, both mentally and physically. It is just *spiritually*, with this problem with the daylight and craving for blood, that I am not so happy with. Too bad it took this curse to give me strength and courage.

"God works in mysterious ways. Remember, your powers just rescued me from a fate worse than death. And you showed your courage *before* you had this new power."

That's right, thinks Schlimazel, a bit proud of himself, even if he did lose round one. "But those *goyim* did have a lesson coming tonight! No offense, of course."

"Watching them run from the big teeth was my favorite part." They cuddle until she falls asleep, cradled in his arms. He caresses her hair and can't help but notice her beautiful, smooth white neck, as his fangs almost seem to grow. Whatever restraint Schlimazel had shown before, *this* was going to be the test of his life. Oy, vey!

Ludmilla awakens after a long sleep, quite refreshed. But the cave is still so dim she cannot tell what time it is. Schlimazel is deep asleep nearby, in his little bed.

She ventures out to find a nice sunny day. The snow has been gone for nearly a week and there is an eruption of wild mountain berries. Butterflies flit about and Ludmilla thanks God for her blessings, for down below lies her former village.

Schlimazel awakens later, after the sun has set. He finds himself wearing a playful ringlet of flowers in his hair that Ludmilla has woven for him. She is doing her best with one of his books and has found the writing tablet he has brought.

"Good morning, Ludmilla."

"Good *evening*, Schlimazel."

They manage like this for a week or so as she soon turns her schedule nocturnal. Her reading is coming along and they even manage a daring burglary one night to get more provisions from the village. This isn't easy, because the superstitious peasants are living in terror and have their places locked up tighter than a drum. "Much of these things have been stolen from Jews, anyway." Reasons Schlimazel.

He manages to hunt, do his own discreet business with the animals and then cook tasty meat recipes for Ludmilla over a makeshift grill, happy as Neanderthals, except that Schlimazel is getting weaker and weaker and weaker.

"What is it, Schly?" As she now calls him. He doesn't want to tell. She hugs him tight and strokes his head, always respectful not to remove his yarmulke. He knows what's happening, but can barely admit it, even to himself. "Whisper it to me, then." And Schlimazel whispers the one thing that he has been dreading. She takes a deep breath. "God has done this for a reason."

"But what am I supposed to do?" Ludmilla looks deep into his eyes, then lays herself languidly across his lap. She slowly pulls her hair aside—to bare her throat.

"If it must be a *person*, to help you stay alive, then take *me!*" Oy vey! And does Schlimazel want a piece of this young lady!

"But I cannot! *No!*" However, his perceptions are too sharp not to have noticed the other thing that he has been avoiding. Ludmilla wants this as well. She is *aching* for it. Almost moaning and writhing for his touch—for his *bite*. Her love for him has somehow been perverted by this strange, demonic magnetism he exudes. Schlimazel caresses her neck and gives it a little kiss. Then a little lick. Oh, so good! *So*, so good. Oy! He wants it *so bad!* But his basic decentness forces him to bolt up, nearly dropping her.

"No! I will not have you like this!" It isn't right! I want to marry you the *proper* way. Even if we must sail the seas and travel the globe, all the way to the colony of New York, where couples of different faiths are said to intermarry!" His strength seems fired up for the first time in days and he is licking his chops. "No, not *your* neck Ludmilla. But some poor *shmuck* in that lousy village down there is going to pay for his sins tonight!"

"OK!" she says, her perky self once again. And the two set off down the mountain.

CHAPTER 7
BOO IT'S THE JEW

THE NIGHT IS WINDY AND CLEAR AS THEY STEAL THEIR WAY INTO Sebreim. Schlimazel and Ludmilla try to decide who is the most evil and deserving, but the village is so damn rotten that it is hard to choose.

"Peotr Slivovich is living on the most land stolen from your Jews."

"His twin sons Olaf and Olag are devils too." Schlimazel recalls a lifetime of taunts and beatings."

"That wench Marishka tells the worst lies about me—but no, it would be sinful to attack her just for that—I suppose."

"There is always Ivan. He is about ready for another Hebrew lesson."

"No, definitely not Marishka. I fear she might enjoy your touch and that I cannot bear."

"That cretin Vladimir is always the one who spills the ale on my head."

"Well if you do bite Marishka, assuming that you think her evil enough, of course, then you must make sure that the teeth really hurt as they pierce the flesh."

And suddenly Michail Shmedlov, one of Ivan's brawny

cohorts, rounds the corner with a bucket of well water and almost bumps into Schlimazel.

"Boo it's the Jew!" yells Schlimazel, doing his fanged bogeyman routine.

Michail screams and drops his bucket. Schlimazel jumps on the larger man and they roll and scuffle as the fledgling vampire tries to find the right spot to bite. But Michail is huge and athletic and manages to land series of punches. And despite his terror—and perhaps through force of habit, he is once again pounding the hell out of Schlimazel, whose strength was sapped to begin with. Ludmilla must clobber the peasant with his bucket in order to subdue him long enough for Schlimazel to go to work. And go to work he does, his fire and energy growing with every drop. After about five or six quarts, Ludmilla tries to restrain her bloodthirsty companion.

"Schlimazel! Enough already!" He is lost in demonic reverie. "You have fed enough! *There is no need to kill him and put more weight on your soul!"* But Schlimazel can't stop. And before the peasant is drained completely, Ludmilla beans her cohort with the sturdy wooden bucket, knocking him off his prey. Schlimazel's eyes are wild and intoxicated. But as the gravity of the act begins to sink in, his emotions do a complete descending arc from his current exhilarated state, to feeling conservatively logical about the event, to a flash of anger at the victim in order to justify things, and finally—the *Fear of God*, with it's ensuing Level Ten Jewish Guilt Attack. Oy! Oy! Oy!

He watches Michail stumble away, yelping like a wounded dog. *"Oy!* What did I do? Did I just do that? *Oy vey!"*

"Come Schly, we must leave." She tries to guide him away.

"Wrath from above should strike me down this instant!"

"You did what you had to. Now let's get out of here!"

Dogs are barking and the screams of women are traveling through the village. *"Oy Vey! Oy veys mir! Oy vey!"*

"Get a hold of yourself."

"Just stand away when the lightening hits! Stand away, I tell you!"

Once back at the cavern, Ludmilla cradles Schlimazel as he rocks in a fetal position. "Maybe at the inn I didn't ask whether the spoon was meat or dairy, that was bad enough. And the animals, *oy*! The animals! But at least we eat animals anyway and what's a little more or less cooking—and I never touched a pig, mind you. But *oy*! Tonight! If we have been given rules of kosher, and eating a little oyster can bring down holy vengeance--then *oy veys mir*! The lightening shall find me in the very back of the cave! And the blood of a *goyim*, yet!"

"Would it be better if you fed on Jews, then, as they eat no pork?"

"You've got to be kidding."

CHAPTER 8
OUR TOWN

Schlimazel wants to survive, if for nothing else, so that he can eventually find a way out of this mess and marry Ludmilla. And after a few days, once he has quieted down and his appetite returns, the two of them settle into a routine of hitting the village several times a week. This also serves as their shopping trip for whatever household items the cavern might need, including some more familiar foods for Ludmilla, like the local cheese and sausages that she is so fond of.

———

But for the villagers, the effect of these nocturnal visits is tumultuous, if not cataclysmic. For as we said earlier, Christianity had come late to these parts, and its roots are not as deep as elsewhere. Superstitions prevail and the fearful peasants go to any length to ward off Schlimazel's attacks. Some wear large crosses, of course. Other try wearing yarmulkes with the Star of David scrawled upon their foreheads as a way of appeasing the *golem*[1]. Some hedge their bets with both crosses and yarmulkes and the Star of David. Of course all the other pagan stuff comes out of the woodwork as well, such as spells, incantations, drum circles, mumbo-jumbo to the tree god, to the sun god or any other deity anyone could recall or invent.

An enormous wicca man is erected in the town square and a fund is begun to construct a golden calf to worship. How ephemeral a thousand years of civilization has become to the village of Sebreim. Eighteenth century Age of Reason stripped back to eighth century Dark Ages in a matter of weeks.

There is even talk of burning all female eccentrics as witches, with Ludmilla's mother and sister heading the list. Fortunately a blabbering blood donor alerts Schlimazel, who makes a point to lower the octane of all the instigators before any real damage can be done.

Schlimazel's victims are all well deserving, of course, and agreed upon beforehand by Ludmilla. They usually recover after a week of zombie-like behavior—followed by occasional fits of paranoid dementia. And it is interesting to note that some of the weaker minded fall into this syndrome without even being bitten, which only feeds the general hysteria.

Ivan briefly organizes a resistance group, who work up the nerve for some daylight forays into the hills, but all it takes is two claps of thunder and the lads are sent tearing through woods, head over heels, back home to the arms of their mothers. Although even home sweet home is not too safe when Schlimazel comes crashing through the roof to drag one of his former tormentors out of bed screaming.

———

Schlimazel is now fit as a fiddle and doing super-human, nightly gymnastic workouts. Ludmilla is becoming a pretty decent reader and even fumbling with her first short story; a fairy tale about a butterfly who wants to marry a moth that has been turned into a spider

She often stays and reads while Schlimazel goes down to feed upon the populace. Too bad that there are so precious few books left in the village. That is one thing the Jews generally take with them. But they did leave behind some nice furnishings and art, which the couple help themselves to, making their cave quite a showcase of interior design. And there is less and less talk of finding a cure and sailing to America.

"Shly."

"Yes, dear."

"Check around for larger wardrobe closet if you have a chance tonight."

"I think the Slobodan's have an extra one they don't deserve."

"Oh, yes, I have seen it. That will do fine."

"Anything else while I'm down there? Some more jams and preserves?"

"Oh, yes! Blackberry. You are always so thoughtful"

Schlimazel readies his boots and checks the sharpness of his teeth.

"You know, Schly—"

"Yes, dear?"

"All things considered, life here is going pretty well for us." Schlimazel almost chokes! For Eastern European Jews have a superstition *never* to boast how well things are doing, at least not so straightforwardly. After thousands of years of persecution, they don't want to provoke *anything*, either from earth or from heaven—Schlimazel, with his luck, especially!

"Don't you *ever* say things like that!"

"Like what? All I said was—"

"All you *meant* to say was, '*Oy*, on Thursday maybe things aren't so bad.'"

"I don't get it."

Schlimazel whispers, "You don't want"—his eyes indicate upwards, "to hear that things are going too well and lightening should strike."

"You people have the strangest ideas."

"You have a *problem* with my people?"

"Just go! Before the sun comes up."

Schlimazel storms down the hill, certain that something is going to happen. The past month has had too much good luck for him. Although what kind of luck is that, he asks. The opportunity to drink blood, then run before getting fried by the sun to a home where he can't have normal conjugal relations?

––––––––––

1. a demon or monster in Jewish stories and myths

CHAPTER 9
MISTER BAD

A FULL MOON IS RISING OVER SEBREIM AND THERE IS TENSION IN the air. Schlimazel walks briskly into the village, irritable, with his jaw well set. Recently some annoying cults have sprung up and a handful of local disenchanted youth mill about a small bonfire near the wicca man.

"O' there *he* is!" says a scrawny, black clad fellow with a primitive ornament pierced through his nose.

His rotund girlfriend cries after Schlimazel, "Take *me*, O' Dark Master! Take *me!*" Schlimazel darts around some houses, not wanting to get involved with these types. His nerves are on edge and he plans to do his business and quickly get home. Then, a familiar sounding voice calls from the shadows.

"Hey Jew!"

Schlimazel, looking not unlike a young Robert De Niro in the moonlight, replies back, "Are you talking to me?"

It is Ivan, wearing a ridiculous wizard's gown. "I am not afraid!

My magic powder shall disarm you!"

"Are you talking to me!?"

Ivan throws a handful of powdered chalk in Schlimazel's

face, making him cough. He responds by punching Ivan in the nose. A brief scuffle ensues and Schlimazel is soon sitting astride Ivan, punching him in the face over and over like boys do in a schoolyard. "Stupid—ignorant—peasant—sheep-*shtooper*[1]," with a punch landing between each word. Ivan's face is bloody and he is crying like a child. Schlimazel gets off him in disgust.

"I shall get you, monster! I shall take her back!" bawls the former bully.

"Tell it to the barnyard!" And Schlimazel continues on. The thought of putting his lips to Ivan's neck just seems too distasteful.

The business with the Slobodans is a messy one. The husband goes so hysterical that Schlimazel can barely hold him still enough to feed. His wife shrieks like a banshee the whole time and tries to fight Schlimazel off by throwing anything in sight, including her famous jams and preserves.

Schlimazel shouts back over her screaming, "Enough already! I'm not killing him, for God sake!" By the time Schlimazel finishes and leaves with the fancy cabinet, which he must literally pry the woman away from, his nerves are shot and he is dripping and sticky.

He manages to avoid those pesky youths in black and trudges off along the dusty road, a bit dwarfed by the furniture he hauls. If only he hadn't been so cross with Ludmilla. The moon is full and he has a bad sickening feeling.

---

1. fornicator

CHAPTER 10
FROM BAD TO WORSE

Up ahead, where the road turns into a steep winding trail, sits the dark coach with the black horses. The carriage is empty! *Oy!* Schlimazel drops his load and races up the hill.

In the cavern he beholds his worst nightmare. The woman with the crimson lips embraces Ludmilla tightly—she is *sucking her blood!*

"*No!*" cries Schlimazel, who leaps with every ounce of strength, and tackles the vampire out of the way. Ludmilla is left sprawling but *thank Heaven* she is still alive! The woman rises up magically, laughing.

"What? You think this is funny!?" screams Schlimazel.

"Hilarious! And I see you've gotten some strength back, darling. You'll be laughing too in another month, after the last attachments to humanity fade."

"What have you done to me!?"

She looks at him admiringly. "I have given you life."

"But why *her*?" Ludmilla lies gasping on the floor.

"Because I was hungry." And with that the woman laughs even harder.

"But why?" He feels his fangs. "Why are we like this?"

"The strong have always fed upon the week. That is nature."

"This is *not* natural. It is abhorrent!"

"You didn't complain the night you suckled my breast."

"You saved my life, yes. And I thank you. Now, please, how do I get back to the way that I was?"

"A wooden stake through the heart, my dear, or maybe a few minutes in the sun."

"I mean, seriously."

"Oh, but I am being serious."

This is even worse than he thought. Oy! "Then who, or *what* are you?"

"A Countess—among other things."

"All right, Countess, your excellency. Thank you again for saving me. But, please, you must *never* touch that girl again. *Never*! She is mine."

"But darling, don't you understand? That *you* are mine. And what is yours, is also mine." Ludmilla stirs. She tries to speak and reaches out for Schlimazel. "Look how pitiful she is. Just get it over with and kill her."

"*Never!*"

"Very well." The Countess hovers over to Ludmilla. Schlimazel leaps furiously to stop her. But she kicks his chin, finishing with an aerial back flip. Schlimazel recovers and leaps at her again and again, but she twirls with a dazzling series of counter attacks. The battle gets more and more surreal, as they kick, twirl, fly and run along the length of the cave. But whatever Schlimazel throws at her, the Countess always prevails. Despite his powers, Schlimazel is left beaten and panting.

"Why me? he asks. "Why me?"

"You, love, have that certain something the ladies want." And a rooster crows. The Countess hovers up, beautiful,

radiant and menacing. "I'll be back the next full moon," she flashes the most beguiling of smiles, "and *then*, till death do us part." Poof! She vanishes. The sound of horses can be heard in the distance. Oy vey! Oy vey! *Oy vey!*

The sun rises over the hills, arcs over the valley and sets across the mountains. And in the cave, Schlimazel feverishly packs things into his new large cabinet. Ludmilla sits at her little desk, zombie-like, scribbling listlessly in the candlelight. Schlimazel is curious and pauses to see what she has written: *The rain in the Ukraine falls mainly on the plain.* Written five thousand times! Oy!

While the night is young, a figure staggers out of the cave with a huge chest on his back, followed by Ludmilla on a leash fashioned from sashes and waistbands. The Polish border is a three days journey, or three nights, in this case, and Schlimazel can only go so fast with his large load and a zombi-fied girlfriend. He is determined to seek proper help; some-thing he should have done the moment the trouble began. The help of a rebbe[1].

Pulling Ludmilla as fast as she can go, they reach the halfway point before sunrise. Schlimazel finds a dense grouping of forest and brush and arranges the chest on its back before crawling inside with Ludmilla. Things should be safe and dark enough. And they are undisturbed as the day passes, except for a brown bear sniffing around a bit, then peeing on their furniture.

They make good progress the next night and approach a small border checkpoint shortly before dawn. A guard is asleep in his little kiosk. Schlimazel tries to slip past. "Where are you going at this hour?"

"Nowhere," answers Schlimazel, not feeling particularly clever. The guard can't help but notice the yarmulke and a tied-up gentile girl. This is going to mean serious money.

"You had better have a pot of gold, Jew, or I am taking you to the prefecture." Schlimazel can't resist his tough guy act. He puts down his load and turns to he guard.

"Are you talking to me!?"

"Yes, I am talking to you!"

"Are you talking to me!?"

"Who do you think I am talking to, insolent filth!"

Schlimazel makes a quick meal of the fellow before moving on.

---

1. rabbi

CHAPTER II
THE GOLEM'S GOLEM

THE LITTLE TOWN OF GROZNYK HAS A YESHIVA THAT SCHLIMAZEL attended briefly as a boy. He remembers Rebbe Plotnik, who lived with his wife in a little cottage. The lights are on and smoke comes from the chimney. Schlimazel hides his load and removes the leash from Ludmilla, taking her by the hand.

———

"Good evening Rebbe."

"Schlimazel!? Is that *you*? All grown up? It's been maybe twelve years since that day of your dropping the scrolls. I didn't think I'd see you back so soon."

"I am very sorry about that, but please rebbe, I have another matter, of the gravest importance, and I need your wise and learned counsel.

"Counsel that cannot wait until morning?" Schlimazel seems terribly anxious. The rebbe's wife looks at them with suspicion, but—"Please come in," says the rebbe, who is still a rebbe, even at this hour. "Gittle, get our guests some tea!" His wife spits three times and walks off brusquely.

"Thank you Rebbe Plotnik."

"Now, in a *concise* manner, what is it that cannot wait until tomorrow?"

Schlimazel doesn't know where to start.

"Well Rebbe, about a month ago, these *goyim* were beating me within an inch of my life and I was thrown to die in the snow—"

"*Oy!*" interjects the bearded scholar.

"And I was frozen like ice as my life was flashing before me—including that unfortunate incident with the scrolls."

"*Oy.*"

"And a beautiful Countess in a black coach rescued me—and to save my life..."

"I'm listening."

Schlimazel hurries to finish his story. "And to save my life, she sucked my blood and made me drink some of hers so I cannot stay in the sun anymore and need to drink blood myself. *Oy!* And now the Countess has bitten my fiancee and turned her into a drooling *shmendrik* for a week, that is usually how long it lasts. You see I rescued Ludmilla from her rotten husband and now we want to marry, but not until this terrible curse is lifted. So please, Rebbe, what should I do?"

The rebbe sits and looks at him—obviously the boy has gone totally *meshuggeneh*. His wife returns with a pot of tea, just in time to watch Schlimazel *demonstrate his fangs!* She screams and drops the kettle! "*Oy!*" says the terrified rebbe, undergoing a very rapid reality adjustment. "A golem's *golem*! Here to punish me! For expelling him from the yeshiva!"

"No, rebbe, *no*! All I want is to lift this curse and live a righteous life—I swear, on all that is Holy!" The rebbe reflexively spouts a quick protective blessing in Hebrew that his terrified wife adds *amen* to.

"*Oy!* If it were only the *shicksa*[1] needing a divorce, *Oy!* That alone would be complicated enough. But this golem business and the biting of the necks? For that, my poor son, we will need a more learned rebbe than I."

"The rain, in the Ukraine, falls mainly, on the plain," mutters Ludmilla vacantly.

"Don't mind her," counsels Schlimazel.

"Wait! Wait! My beloved teacher, Rebbe Israel Baal Shem-Tov, may he rest in peace, had a cousin, also a famous rebbe —*Israel Baal Shlo-Liem!* He was said to be the most learned man of the Kabala, the Jewish Book of Mysticism. *He* would know! In his temple, high up in the mountain, in *Romania,* where they study such things."

"How high in the mountains?" asks his former yeshiva student.

"High," says the rebbe.

———

The journey is long and arduous, and Ludmilla's docile state is now erupting periodically into manic fits of thrashing and gibberish, although Schlimazel prefers even that to the horrible *'rain on the plain in Ukraine,'* business he regrets ever having taught her. But still, the winding trails and virgin hillsides are beautiful, even at night.

He must make one quick refueling stop at a hamlet and is fortunate enough to spy on a man sneaking between two houses—in his nightclothes. Schlimazel intercepts him, assuming the fellow was breaking at least one if not two of the Commandments. Schlimazel leaves the individual with a good few quarts, not wanting to break any of the Commandments himself.

"The rain in the Ukraine falls mainly on the plain."

"Yes, dear," Schlimazel says patiently, as they continue on their quest.

And finally, on the far horizon, shrouded by clouds, high atop a precipitous mountain, Schlimazel sees it. Shlo-Liem Temple! Mecca to the great scholar of the Kabala, master of mysticism and occult phenomena—the esteemed Rebbe, Israel Baal Shlo-Liem! But the sun will soon rise and Schlimazel must make camp for yet another day to pass.

The next evening Schlimazel pulls Ludmilla as fast they can go, climbing and climbing, until just before dawn, when they reach the temple gates. Schlimazel could kiss the ground! Although the place is more rundown than he had pictured. Windows are broken and things seem in disarray. Only the dimmest of lights emanates from within. Schlimazel cannot wait another day and knocks at the temple door. No answer. Then the dim light inside goes out. That is curious? Schlimazel opens the door. The place is seemingly deserted. Very curious!

"*Hello!* Anybody home? Sorry to barge in so late! *Hello!*"

They walk through room after room, many filled with strange charts, dusty books and ancient tomes, but not a sign of life. Suddenly, Ludmilla turns and *screams*! Something scurries into the shadows!

"*Ludmilla?*"

She has apparently snapped out her zombified state.

"Schlimazel! Something was looking in my eyes!"

He sees a movement! A small beast—trying to hide behind the curtains? Schlimazel pulls away the cover—and lo' and behold—a large, old *rat*! *With yarmulke and paysses!*

---

1. Gentile girl

CHAPTER 12
FOLLOW THE YELLOW
BRICK RAT

"Don't hurt me!" it squeaks. "Please!" And Schlimazel had thought he had seen everything!

"Who or *what* in Heaven's name are you?"

"I am called Mac Heath. The good Rebbe--rest his soul--rescued me from a mountain cat and made me his pet."

"Wait a second. What do you mean by, *'rest his soul?'*"

"The beloved Rebbe, Baal Shlo-Liem has passed. Two years ago this month."

"Then where are all the other rebbes and scholars?" asks Schlimazel.

"What other rebbes and scholars? There was only the master and me."

"And now only a rat!?" This is truly the end of Schlimazel's hope. "What's the use I ask you! My luck is so rotten to the core that I might as well give up!"

Ludmilla holds him tight. "Don't worry. I will stand by you no matter what." He kisses her forehead and fights back tears.

Ludmilla whispers to him, "How is it that a rat can talk?"

"That is a long story," responds the rat, who also seems to

have keen sense of hearing. "And I will explain once your mind has rested, as you have obviously just awakened from a *vampire's* bite."

"*Say what!?*" Schlimazel was floored enough just to hear the rat talk. But hitting the nail on the head like this!

"Were you the one who placed the bite?"

"Me! No, *never!*" snaps Schlimazel.

"Perhaps you have managed to keep your good soul then, as the girl is ripe, juicy and tempting—and the two of you seem very much in love."

"This is crazy!" says Schlimazel. "How can a rat talk, let alone know about such things?"

"Miracles happen in strange ways," offers Ludmilla.

"Come," says Mac Heath, "I will lead you to blankets and a dark room."

"That is kind of you, little rat."

"I don't get it?" mumbles Schlimazel.

"This is Transylvania," responds the rat Mac Heath, leading the way along dark and musty corridors.

———

The following evening they sit at a table illuminated by a single candle. Some fruit, nuts and berries have been set upon a tray for Ludmilla, who shows quite an appetite after her ordeal. Little Mac Heath sits perched on a high stool so he can reach the table and nibble a bit from his own small tray.

"So how did the Rebbe pass? Was it these same blood suckers who have infected me?" asks Schlimazel

"No, it was not vampires," says the rat. "I think it was too much of the fatty foods he liked so much and not enough fruits and vegetables."

"But it is well known that one needs fatty foods to stay

plump and warm for the winter," instructs Ludmilla, looking quite svelte despite a few strategically placed curves.

Mac Heath winks to Schlimazel before quoting some Shakespeare, *"Beauty itself doth of itself persuade the eyes of men without an orator."* Ludmilla blushes and smiles coyly as Schlimazel looks on incredulously, barely believing his eyes and ears.

"So tell me, Mister Rat named Mac Heath who quotes from William Shakespeare. What can you tell us about *vampires*?"

"*Oy!* Vampires. Also known as *nosferatu*. The *golem* of the *goyim*. They have plagued these Carpathian mountains since the dawn of history."

"And never a *Yiddishe* vampire?" asks our fanged, yarmulked hero.

"There were a few, but no longer. Although now there is *you*, my unfortunate friend. The Rebbe was studying this very phenomena when his great heart failed him."

"And not from the fatty foods, mind you," chimes Ludmilla.

"*Shoosh*, darling. Let our miracle rat tell us what he knows."

Mac Heath's little voice gets more serious. "Well, as you must be aware, vampires feed on the blood of the living and cannot bear the divine light of the sun's rays." Schlimazel lowers his eyes. "And they are almost indestructible."

"A wooden stake through the heart?" Schlimazel grins ironically.

"Yes, as well as sunlight. Also fire can destroy them, although that takes a while. And the loss of all the blood to another vampire, a perversity they sometimes exhibit."

"And how do they get their power?" asks Ludmilla.

"As soon as the spell is cast, from exchanging of the blood,

At the end of a grueling week, Mac Heath does a final analysis of his equations. He removes his tiny spectacles and rubs his tired, red, beady eyes. "Schlimazel, my lad—"

"Yes, master," as Schlimazel now addresses his teacher, showing proper deference.

"I hate to tell you this, but luck is not on your side."

"No kidding!" says Schlimazel.

"Seriously, though—after all this work, we have managed to increase your strength and abilities only marginally. This Countess you speak of can not only fly circles around you, but she will have the ability to cloud your mind and influence your thoughts. And the longer you wait to destroy her, the greater her evil power shall grow over you."

"What are you saying? That hope is lost?"

"There is always the faith that after the stake pierces your heart—and the *sooner the better*—that a righteous soul might still be allowed into the kingdom of Heaven."

Schlimazel is grateful for that, of course, but before he departs this good green earth, he was hoping to enjoy at least a few good years with his one true love.

"My luck!" cries Schlimazel. "So this is it! Game over! Schlimazel loses again! Fetch the wooden stake. We might as well get it over with, before my mind becomes further infected and who knows what deeds I might do."

"Wait," says Ludmilla. "What if he had an *ally* to battle the Countess?"

"An ally?" asks the little master. "And who might that be?"

"Me." says Ludmilla calmly.

"But you would not last a minute against a vampire, sweet child."

"What if I were *also* a vampire, with the power to leap and fly?"

"*Forget it!*" says Schlimazel. "I would never allow that!"

"I will not let you perish without a fight, Schly! I will battle that evil woman, whether I have special powers or not! At least we will go together!"

"But Ludmilla, darling. Even if we do manage to vanquish the foul bitch, it is by no means assured that we will ever return to our normal states. Isn't that right, master?"

"Yes—but I am working on it!" says the wise and optimistic rat. "But do not even think of becoming a vampire, my girl!" Mac Heath sternly admonishes Ludmilla. "For it is the curse of Hell itself! Hell itself!"

"*Oy!*" Says Schlimazel.

"Okay, look what I have found in the library!" Ludmilla produces a dusty old tome.

Shao Lin Gong Foo, by Master Wing-Lin *Wang*, reads the title in Mandarin, which they do not understand. But the detailed, step-by-step fighting illustrations are easy enough.

"We shall study this, then." says Mac Heath.

CHAPTER 13
THE DREAM TEAM

LATER THAT NIGHT, BEFORE THE SUN COMES UP, LUDMILLA AND Schlimazel cuddle together in their cozy, windowless room. They pour over the *gong foo* book, marveling at the impressive drawings and diagrams.

"If I would have given that woman a punch like this, she would not have smiled so much!" Schlimazel is playing the fight over in his head.

"And the nerve of the foul bitch, taking my blood like that!" Ludmilla steams. "The only one to take anything from me—will be you." Schlimazel looks kindly on her. What a brave and noble heart this girl has. And Ludmilla looks back at Schlimazel, filled with love and admiration. "Shly?"

"Yes dear?"

She mischievously rolls atop him. "You have not kissed me, not once since that night in the tavern."

He pauses. "I know. I have been afraid of what might happen."

She slowly puts her lips a hair-breadth from his, and whispers, "Like what?" A long and excruciatingly delicious pause—

"This," and he kisses Ludmilla. Deliriously. Passionately. And he rolls atop of her.

She softly moans to him, "Shly, it is okay. Take me, now. Do it!" Schlimazel's knee is pressed between her aching thighs. He trails his lips sensually down her neck. "Do it. Do it to me now," she gasps, breathlessly.

Delicately, he bites her neck. An animal virility courses through his body as she writhes and moans beneath him—as Schlimazel tenderly drinks her blood. Finally, he pulls back, not entirely sure of what he has just done.

"Did I hurt you?" He asks.

Ludmilla opens her eyes and smiles weakly. "Oh my!" she sighs, "I am a maiden, but I think I just had one of those 'explosions of pleasure' the older girls speak of." She manages to roll atop Schlimazel. He is glowing with happiness, life and charisma—the guilt will come later. "Now it is my turn!" she says, scratching his neck with a small knife and putting her lips to the mark.

"No, Ludmilla. No my love. You do not know what you are doing!"

"Yes, I do." She holds her mouth firm to his neck. Schlimazel does not resist, praying that this is somehow for the greater good, as Ludmilla's breath grows faster and faster, the pupils of her eyes grow large. A warm blackness envelops the room, with swirls of crimson red falling through infinite space, then soaring—higher, and higher, and higher.

———

A rooster crows. Sunlight fills the temple courtyard as Mac Heath stumbles out in his threadbare little night shirt and a tiny night cap over his yarmulke. *"Oy!"* He turns to Heaven.

"May Heaven give me the strength and wisdom to finish what I have set in motion!" And the furry rat scrambles off to work.

Mac Heath sits in his study, squinting over large, dusty volumes as the sun sets once again over the ancient hills of Transylvania. Enter Schlimazel, looking more than a little guilty, his jaw set, grim and determined. He slaps the *Gong Foo* book down, straps on all the lead weights, and climbs the ladder. Mac Heath studies the illustrations in the *Gong Foo* book. He apparently had overlooked this volume, perhaps due to the unintelligible cover, he surmises. Or maybe he is just getting old.

"Ouch!" cries Schlimazel, more resolute than ever to slow his rate of descent—or bash his brains out in the process.

———

Eight hours later the rat shouts at Schlimazel, "Faster, you lazy boy! Faster I say!" Schlimazel is performing a long sequence of kicks, twirls, leaps and punches, right from the *Gong Foo* book, only to wend back through the same motions in perfect *reverse*. Then forward again. And so on. "Faster, you dropper of the scrolls! *Save future victims from her Curse!*"

Finally Schlimazel stops. "I cannot take it anymore." He is covered with bruises. Then suddenly, an airborne form arcs across the room and hits him square in the chest with both feet. *Oof!* It's Ludmilla! She crashes and tumbles, not used to her new strength. She laughs at the sight of this. "Ludmilla!" cries Schlimazel. "You are awake!"

"And that isn't all I am." She jumps in a complete flip and lands on her feet. Ludmilla breaks a smile, revealing her new set of fangs.

"Oy!" Cries Mac Heath. "What have you done?!"

Schlimazel cowers guiltily.

"It was my choice! My choice! I shall support the team!" says Ludmilla, beaming with determination and a new vitality.

Mac Heath cries "No! No! No! You silly girl! You stupid boy!" He rages about, shaking his paws in the air and sputtering Hebrew prayers, punctuated by the ritualistic spitting three times—that Jews do when trying to ward off evil. "And it will take more than jumping tricks to stop an evil Countess from making playthings of you!" He goes on with a bit more ritual spitting and anguished prayers until finally, resigned, he points to the cursed ladder. Ludmilla dutifully ascends as the rat fiddles with his time piece and velocity chart, muttering "Oy veys mir..."

———

Hours later, just before sunrise, Schlimazel and Ludmilla curl up for a day's rest. "I don't feel so invincible," says Ludmilla, nursing an aching head.

"Don't worry." assures Schlimazel, "things seem to heal up while you are sleeping. It is really quite amazing."

"I just pray that we survive this without our souls burning in Hell for all eternity."

"*Oy!*" Says the world's only Jewish vampire.

———

When the sun sets the following evening and the moon begins to rise, Mac Heath stands outside the temple gates and admonishes his pupils. "Do what you have to, in order to preserve your strength, but do no more than that! Always avoid killing! And select a target so evil that you are doing his neighbors a favor, even if it lasts only for a week!"

"Yes, master!" Reply Schlimazel and Ludmilla.

"And hurry right back as soon as you are finished. Our time is growing short!"

The duo bound down the mountain like happy children. They skip and leap together, holding hands and laughing at their magically long strides. Although the future is fraught with peril, this night is theirs!

"If only we could be like this without having to feed on the blood of humans!" notes Ludmilla.

"I know!" chimes Schlimazel. "This is the best I have ever felt!" Yes, life has its moments, however ironic and fleeting— and in the distance, the sound of rollicking music.

————

Schlimazel and Ludmilla crouch like beasts of prey in the hills overlooking a small gypsy encampment. A handful of colorful men and women sit around a fire as a passionate fellow sings to the accompaniment of violins and various instruments.

"I never thought I would crave it so," says Ludmilla, licking her lips.

"You have *no* idea!" answers her fangsome friend.

"And you have been such a gentleman all this time, never trying to bite me at night!"

"Thank you for that, Ludmilla." This means a lot to Schlimazel.

"Shall we pounce on them now?"

"Wait, we must only find evil ones." He replies.

And here they come. Two armed, uniformed militiamen, flanked by six hulking, club wielding peasants. None of the men appear to be older than twenty. The Gypsy music stops and women are rushed inside a covered wagon.

"You thieving scum are not permitted in this land!" barks a militiaman.

"We are just leaving, your excellency," says the gypsy elder.

"Not so fast!" replies the soldier, wielding his gun.

"We will pay tribute, of course!" interjects the old man. The peasant thugs chuckle and snicker. They are drunk and out for mischief.

"I want the red skirt!" a pimple faced youth chortles to his cohorts.

"Leave the women alone, I beg you! We have gold!" The old man fumbles for some coins, his hands so nervous that he drops them in the dirt. The poor fellow is terrified for his daughters and scrambles to retrieve the money. Someone boots his rear and sends him sprawling. The thugs really find this hilarious. Until—

"Which one of you walking shit-piles wants your weapon shoved up his ass first? Schlimazel steps out of the shadows, cool as can be. The bullies are at first too surprised to speak. And from a *Jew*, yet!

"I will teach a Jew how to talk!" shouts a militiaman, raising his musket to blow Schlimazel's brains out. *THWACK!* The gun is sent flying by a spinning kick, leaving the soldier looking stupidly at his empty stinging hands. He rages and sputters, "You will pay *slowly* then, Jew—" *CRACK! POW! KICK! PUNCH! SMACK!*

The fellow is punched, kicked, and smacked backwards so hard and so fast, that he is sent rolling and tumbling head over heels. When he comes to an eventual halt, one can almost hear the sound of little birds tweeting. Schlimazel bounces around like a cocky Bruce Lee. The other militiaman takes aim to fire, when, *THWOMP!* Ludmilla drops from a tree, *head first*, landing cranium to cranium, crunching the militiaman to the ground. He lies there dazed as she springs up, all smiles. The gypsies are impressed, to say the least. And with the guns out of action, the rest of the bully boys seem to be losing a bit of their bravado, particularly as a few emboldened gypsies produce knives.

"What's the matter, pork boys? Not so brave without your husbands to defend you?" jibes Schlimazel.

"Hello, walking buckets of shit!" Ludmilla says. "Is *my* skirt to your liking, even though it is not red?" Ludmilla manages a long sweeping slap that catches three faces, before cracking their heads together. "What a bunch of *shmen-derikies! Ha!"*

Schlimazel turns to the other three. "What was that you said?" They shake their heads nervously. Schlimazel has had too much practice at the receiving end of this sort of thing. He pushes one in the chest. "Hey! I'm talking to *you,* pimpled face!"

"But I did not say anything!"

"What was that you said!?"

"But, but, I did not say—" THUD-THUD-THUD! Three devastating punches to three midsections and the trio double over with the wind knocked out of them. Gypsies whistle and jeer as the thugs clutch their stomachs. Schlimazel advances on the staggering bullies, who back away like timid boys.

"BOO!" Schlimazel does the bogeyman; arms raised and *fangs bared viciously.*

"Yaaa!" And six burly peasants, attitudes thoroughly adjusted, run screaming into the night. A few can be heard crashing into trees. Schlimazel and Ludmilla convulse with tears of laughter. But the appearance of these large incisors have not been lost on the gypsies either, who now edge back in fear.

Schlimazel and Ludmilla drag the two dazed militiamen into the darkness of the woods for a quick feeding.

They emerge a few minutes later to find the gypsy elder, his hands clutching precious gold coins.

"Please! Take this offering, for your kind help. Then let us go in peace!"

"Don't worry, sir, we would never hurt you or your people," says Ludmilla.

"It will bring bad luck not to pay you. You must take the money!" The nervous elder holds out the coins.

"Don't worry about it," says Schlimazel.

"Pay us by playing your beautiful music, then!" suggests Ludmilla.

"Excellent suggestion, pay us with music!" says Schlimazel.

After a brief huddle the gypsies begin to sing and play like their lives depended on it.

The night is clear and the heavens filled with stars. Schlimazel breathes deep and looks at Ludmilla. She is lit radiantly by the campfire. The music is intoxicating. He takes her up to dance. And dance they do--with super-human leaps and dips and dizzying twirls. Gypsies gather round to watch.

The night is magical. Gypsies drink wine from leather flasks and display their own incredible dancing to their visitors' delight. They create verses about an evening that future generations will long sing of.

♪ *"Sing 'O noble Gypsies, who travel the land about. Remember the*
Yiddishe vampire night,
How they chased those shit-boys out!" ♫

By the time the first sign of dawn approaches, the gypsies have crossed the Hungarian border—and Schlimazel and

Ludmilla have barely made it back to the temple. They laugh and sing and merrily hold hands. What a delirious night this has been! But the front door is firmly locked. And just to the side of it, Mac Heaths stands glaring on the window sill. "Where have you been!?"

"Doing as you told us, master," offers Ludmilla.

"I did not tell you to dawdle the night and make a *game* of this!"

"The victims were *really* bad," assures Schlimazel, suppressing a grin.

"Look at you! Grinning, having fun, staying out and forgetting the task at hand!"

"But—"

"Shut your mouth!" screams the rat. "The blood of your fellow man, filling your gut! And you *smile*? In violation of all that is kosher and holy!?"

Ludmilla chimes in, "But we were just—"

"Silence!" You, a Christian girl, no less, who has just willingly tarnished her soul--should find this act repulsive! Instead you grin with blood on your clothing. *Blood!* What a mockery you make of the blood that your savior, Jesus Christ, shed for you upon the cross!"

Ludmilla did feast on her militiaman quite easily, and really enjoyed it—a fact that now causes her great shame.

Mac Heath is in a righteous rage. "You both should have returned *six hours ago!* For every minute we lose, the *evil* draws you closer! After the moon is full again, all may be lost! *Do you understand!? Do you understand me!?"* The fervent rat is working himself into quite a dither. *"The evil!* The cursed *evil,* the *unholy evil,* that draws you closer and closer!

Do you understand me!?" Spittle is flying off his furry mouth as he paces and rants. *"The evil! Do you understand!? The cursed evil! Do you understand me!?"*

"Yes, master! Yes master! We understand! We understand!" Plead the guilty duo, nervous and aware that dawn is breaking. "Please, sir, may we must just go in now?"

"*No!* You shall stand out there. I *forbid* you in this holy temple!"

The first rays of light! "Master, *please!*" The vampires are getting *really* hot.

"*No! I forbid it! I forbid it!*" says the little rat, his voice hoarse and spent. Steam is rising off of the couple. Ludmilla is crying hysterically. Finally, "All right, come in then. But the only *game* shall be returning your souls to *righteousness!*"

"Amen!" shout Schlimazel and Ludmilla, scrambling in before they fry.

———

Back inside their dark little room, after they manage to cool down a bit, Schlimazel grumbles to Ludmilla, "Oy, did they teach that rat to *talk!* What a mouth he has on him!"

"And did you see all the spits fly off from his muzzle?"

"Half of them hit me in the eye!"

"One of them landed on my lips!" she grimaces.

"*Ewww!*" say the two of them, hugging and giggling once again. It is well that they soon got a good day's sleep, as it was certain the next night would be a tough one.

———

And it is! Mac Heath works them with a holy vengeance. Over and over and over, Ludmilla is run through every move in the *Gong Foo* book with Schlimazel acting as her sparring foil. The rat screams and curses like an insane little drill sergeant.

"Harder! Faster! Slower! Not like that! *Idiots!* Faster! Slower! *Faster!*"

They are quite beat up by the end of the night, but Ludmilla seems to be learning. And Schlimazel's own fighting confidence is greater than ever. Despite a hundred bruises that his erstwhile better half has just inflicted upon him, he volunteers a fully leaded climb up the ladder, to cap off the evening. "Watch me, now, master, as I shall slow it to a *stop!*" And Schlimazel does a Bruce Lee cry and dives off head first, until the hard stone floor does in fact, bring him to a stop. The rooster crows and they call it a night.

———

The next week is like an eternity of pain and effort. Schlimazel and Ludmilla drill, both as sparring opponents, and then as a highly efficient fighting team. Their power seems to grow and their magical, flying leaps are becoming more and more impressive.

The duo execute a particularly beautiful series of partner moves, running along walls, leaping great distances, sailing through the air, all the while helping and propelling the other. "The Moscow ballet will be quite impressed," comments the rat, "but the Countess may not!"

And thus the next stage of their training begins. Working with wooden stakes! For that is what this is all about. Mac Heath has them drive and throw wooden stakes in a thousand different ways. They are even drilled in the improvisation of creating stakes from anything handy, and much of the furniture starts to disappear, stick by stick.

Finally, Schlimazel ties on his leaden weights and trudges up the ladder. Mac Heath readies his time piece. Ludmilla holds her breath and—

He dives off, sails downward, and just inches from the floor, Schlimazel *hovers*, bouncing ever so slightly, like an invisible bunjee chord holds his legs. Ludmilla and Mac Heath clap and applaud. Schlimazel is crying like Bruce Lee and using all his intention to not only stay above the ground, but to actually *rise back up again!* Until his cosmic chord snaps and he lands thudding on his head.

Later, Schlimazel and Ludmilla snuggle up for sleep as the dawn rises outside.

"So what about the Section Two, where they turn us back into normal humans?" she wonders.

"That's what I was thinking," says Schlimazel.

"I am afraid of how good it tasted."

"I sure hope that rat knows what he's doing."

"From a simple peasant girl, my life sure has taken the interesting twists."

"Like having fangs and lying in bed with a Jewish vampire?"

"Yes, for example."

"You are definitely an odd one, Ludmilla." He strokes her affectionately.

"You are pretty odd, too. But in the way that I like." They curl up and go to sleep.

CHAPTER 14
FIDDLER ON THE RAT

MAC HEATH, ON THE OTHER HAND, HAS GONE INTO OVERDRIVE. He frantically pours through books, scrolls, charts and volume after volume of the Rebbe's notes. If only he had spent less time on the ladder trick and more time on the vampire reversal trick! Oy! His eyes burn and his head is killing him. But he only continues at a more furious pace. For it was *he* that the poor *Schlimazel*, so aptly named, came to for help and it was Mac Heath who encouraged the sweet gentile girl to sacrifice, perhaps, her eternal soul!

———

Hours later, as the sun starts to set, Mac Heath takes off his tiny spectacles to rub his aching eyes. At that moment, he feels like a very old rat. But no time for self pity! He puts his glasses back on and turns another page, written by some ancient Talmudic scholar. And *there* it is! Along with notes and comments in Rebbe Shlo-Liem's own hand! *This* is the missing piece that deals with a specific form of demonic exorcism—*the one that handles vampires!* The good Rebbe, may God rest his soul, was only waiting for the *right* vampires to walk in, so he could perform the ritual and prove his hypothesis. Mac Heath is so relieved that emotion overwhelms him and he breaks into sobbing tears.

———

Schlimazel and Ludmilla have just awakened and walk hurriedly to the large study that has served as their gymnasium. "I wonder what the little czar has planned for us tonight?" she ponders.

"Flattening our heads, I'm sure," he replies. As they approach the study, they are surprised to hear Mac Heath's voice—*singing?*

♪ *"Hidle deedle Hi Dee! If I was a rich rat,*
Hidee hidle deedee hidle deedle dum!"

The rat is dancing on the table like a little Reb Tevye and a wine bottle sits half empty! *"Master?"* Call an incredulous Schlimazel and Ludmilla. Mac Heath is lost in reverie, front paws held high, shuffling joyously, composing melodies, *direct from the soul*—as is encouraged by Rebbe Shlo-Liem's more famous cousin, the esteemed Baal Shem-Tov and his burgeoning new *Chassidic* movement, which is sweeping the land at this time.

"All I'd do is piddee piddee pum,
If I was wealthy rat! Oy!
Hidle deedle Di Dum—" ♫

Schlimazel and Ludmilla come to the table. "Master? Are you all right?" Mac Heath shimmies over, brimming with joy and happiness.

"Ah, my boy, Schlimazel! And *Ludi*! *Mien shayne*[1] *Ludles*. Come closer, children, so that I may see you!" They reach their heads near and Mac Heath gives each of their noses a big kiss.

"Shouldn't we be training now?" asks Schlimazel.

"Enough of the jumping around. Take a moment for prayer and contemplation. Confess your sins. And if the spirit moves you, then by all means, *let it spring forth*—as I do!" And Mac Heath starts to sing and shimmy around the table again.

"But *last week* you told us—" Ludmilla is shushed by Schlimazel.

"What about the Second Part, master? Turning us back to normal."

"You just worry about Part One!" says Mac Heath, "And *hurry!*" and he passes out in a blissful stupor.

———

Schlimazel trudges down the hill with the trusty old closet on his back. Ludmilla dances along, doing her rather gentile version of Chassidic spontaneous singing: *"Hi-dee hi-dee Ho! Tra-la-la, tra-la-la! If I were the richest girl! Tra la la!"*

"Must you do that now?" Schlimazel is worried and on edge.

"Do you think that I am not worried as well?" she snaps. "I am only trying to let the *'spirit spring forth,'* as the master instructed us!" Schlimazel flashes her a really hard look and she immediately becomes subservient. Almost zombie like.

"*Oy!*" cries Schlimazel, taking her hand and doubling their pace.

The night ends with a miserable meal of wild rodent in the pouring rain. Ludmilla looks at the face of her dead prey and winces. Guess who it looks like?

"I was thinking the same thing," says Schlimazel, tossing his animal away in disgust. They climb into their dank closet, painfully aware that it isn't the least bit waterproof.

————

The next night they bound along quickly and finally make the Ukraine border. There are two burly guards stationed at the little outpost, drunk on the job and snoring. They will awaken from zombified states—surprised to say the least, about a week later. And neither will imbibe a drop at work for the rest of their lives.

The meal nourishes our protagonists, who push along at an even faster pace. The moon is waxing large, but still a few nights shy of full. Schlimazel and Ludmilla must bed down one last time before reaching their destination. They chat a bit in the darkness of their musty closet.

"Schly?"

"Yes dear."

"Do you love me?"

"Yes, Ludmilla. Very much."

"Then I will change your luck!"

Schlimazel looks at her sweet, innocent face, bloody fangs not withstanding, hoping and praying that she is right.

————

The next evening, as the moon looms really large, they discard their load and take a superhuman shortcut along the very crest of the mountain. Even the wolves are amazed to see the ghostly silhouettes, skipping and singing, illuminated by the eerie light.

"Oy yoy doy dum, deedle deedle, doy dum—"
"Tra-la, tra-la, tra-la! Tra la la la!"

The wolves prefer Schlimazel's singing to hers. Perhaps it's his ethnic inflection.

———

And across the hills they go, further and further, until they see, in a valley far below, the place of their birth—and hopefully, not their death. The dirty little village of Sebriem. The sun will rise shortly and the two take refuge in their old cave.

———

Inside the cavern, Schlimazel fashions some sharp wooden stakes while Ludmilla shakes the dust off some sheets. They are dead tired yet have a very uneasy feeling. "Maybe we should stay awake," she says. "What if that woman comes in our sleep?"

"She'd be risking the sun—although with *my* luck, anything's possible."

"What if we kill her and the master still cannot change us back?"

"That would be *really* bad. I don't even want to think about it!"

"Maybe we could hire ourselves out, like mercenary soldiers that are in love, but who only fight in the night."

"You get some funny ideas, Ludmilla."
"It is a book that I am planning to write, in any case."
"Oh."

---

1. my beautiful

CHAPTER 15

STRANGERS IN THE NIGHT

THEY DECIDE TO SLEEP IN SHIFTS. BUT IT IS HARD. SCHLIMAZEL sits up in bed, armed with his wooden stakes. His head keeps nodding and nodding. Oy! His mind is wandering. Rats, *gong foo*, gypsy music. Ludmilla is sleeping like a log. Eventually, Schlimazel's chin is touching his chest.

That is when he slips into a profound Blackness. Insinuated by swirls of crimson. And pounding hooves. Taking him through the night. Faster and faster. High above the trees, above the clouds. The night is warm and inviting. Dark, dark blue, with soft tinges of orange. Schlimazel flies high above the earth. Orange becomes red. And redder. Until the whole universe is crimson. The feeling is ecstatic, surreal, and time seems to almost stand still. The intense crimson is broken by a whiteness. A living, breathing, satiny whiteness. It is Ludmilla's naked flesh.

Their bodies float together in the slowest of motion. A feeling of overwhelming passion. As fangs pierce into necks. The ecstasy grows. And as it reaches its climax, Schlimazel is suddenly aware that it is not Ludmilla's eyes looking back into his—but the *Countess*! She laughs maniacally. He panics

73

and grabs a stake to push against her chest. A piercing scream! Schlimazel pulls back in horror! He is in bed with Ludmilla! Bloody marks are on her neck. He holds a stake sharply against her chest.

"Oh, my God!" Ludmilla cries hysterically. Schlimazel casts the stake away and hugs her tight. Blood is on his lips.

"I dreamed it was her!" cries Schlimazel. "Something *terrible* came over me! And something has come into the cave as well!"

While they were asleep, the cavern was *totally redecorated* with items taken from Ludmilla's old room, as well as stinking, soiled laundry—dank with mildew. It was the last load that Schlimazel had walked away from! A wolf howls as night descends with an ironic sense humor, although neither Schlimazel nor Ludmilla find it funny, as they grab some stakes and quickly search the cavern. Not a soul. Not even a bat. With the sun-light almost faded, they peer out the entrance.

In the distance, trudging down the hill, is a pack of peasant zombies. A girl turns back and smiles robotically. It is Ludmilla's sister! It's no wonder the rebbe never made it past Part One.

———————

Schlimazel and Ludmilla run about the cave in a panic, she screaming, him blabbering a chorus of '*oys*'. They finally manage to channel their shouting into a brief round of spontaneous Chassidic song, as their master counseled, until feeling totally ridiculous and simply huddling together in fear. After a while, Schlimazel gains control of himself and notes grimly, "I guess it's time to kill the bitch."

"Just don't get us mixed up again!" warns Ludmilla, checking her neck wounds.

"*Oy!* I should rather shove the stake up my own ass!"

"I will help you if you try that again."

"Really?"

"No. I am only making a joke."

Schlimazel goes into hyper drive, fashioning stakes, as well as some other creative little weapons while Ludmilla works quickly from a box of thread and fabrics.

CHAPTER 16

THE LION DON'T SLEEP TONIGHT

In the village, the quiet village—zombified peasants walk about under the moonlight. Some perform basic tasks, like building crude additions to a towering, spastic looking wicca man. Others just trudge about with less sense of purpose, bumping into things or each other. And barely discernible in the night, two black-clad, masked and hooded figures slip over a wall, appearing almost *ninja*-like—although one of the hoods has a yarmulke sewn onto it. The figures dart silently from shadow to shadow.

"We must try to not kill the villagers," whispers Schlimazel.

"Well don't worry about it if that sister of mine gets in your way."

"The rat warned us not to destroy the innocent."

"Did you see the look that little wench gave me?"

"You should meet my brother."

They dart around from shadow to shadow some more, confidant that their stealth and disguise is working. Until someone bangs their heads together and pulls their masks off. It is the Countess! She laughs as the duo stagger trying to clear their heads. Schlimazel reflexively bounces back, wielding a sharp wooden stake, but the powerful vampire flips effortlessly away.

"You think we are your playthings!?" cries Schlimazel, holding his head.

"Yes."

Ludmilla throws a stake at blurring speed. The Countess snatches it from the air, does a cartwheel and throws it back even *faster*. Our heroine barely dodges her ass out of the path of a whistling spear—obviously not aimed at the heart.

"She will always be a peasant, darling," jibes the Countess. "Even as a vampire her ass will swell so large that you will eventually think it was her mother!"

"Watch who you are talking to," Ludmilla says, "cheap wench but with expensive clothes—which barely conceal an ass *much* more fat and sagging than my own!" And Ludmilla bounds furiously, head over heels, towards the Countess.

"Wait up!" Schlimazel joins her a millisecond later.

They fly at the Countess feet first. The Countess deftly parries and rolls away. A brief but intense two on one battle ensues. Schlimazel and Ludmilla jump, kick, punch, run along walls and fly in the air. But the Countess gracefully fends off every attack. And when she counter attacks, it is shattering. Our duo are beaten, kicked and punched. But somehow, they manage to employ greater and greater teamwork until the battle soon becomes a whizzing, furious and quite balletic stalemate.

The contestants pull back for a quick breather. "You, or someone, has taught the tramp well," pants the Countess.

"Be careful who you call the tramp—*you*, who pull your bosoms out for every passing Igor, Boris or Ivan to suck a little from!"

"Well you should have seen the smile on this one's lips,"

the Countess eyes Schlimazel, "while I caressed his manhood as *he* suckled!"

"*Not true!* I don't remember that at all!" he shouts. Ludmilla looks at Schlimazel plaintively. "If it did happen, I was a victim of circumstances, then!"

"Enough already! My poor, little 'victim of circumstances.'" The Countess focuses laser sharp on Schlimazel. *"Now kill her!"* Something is taking hold of his mind, digging its way in, deep and fast.

"*Schly!*" cries Ludmilla. Whatever is infecting his head, is also permeating her own.

"*No!*" screams Schlimazel. He concentrates to center himself, then shudders as he expels some foreign energy—and then, with a defiant little Bruce Lee hoop and a hop, Schlimazel flies at the Countess! "*Yaaaah!*"

"*Yaaaah!*" cries Ludmilla, lunging forth as well. This time the duo attack with a greater ferocity and purpose. The Countess spins, kicks, parries and swings, but Schlimazel and Ludmilla are now starting to land some blows. The fight is taking larger and more magical proportions as the battle carries them up trees and over roofs. The Countess fights back even more fiercely, but the duo are in sync like finely attuned dancers and assault the Countess with devastating effectiveness. Finally, in a blurring hyper speed, Schlimazel and Ludmilla deliver a stunning offense that sends the Countess flying into a wall, beaten and staggered.

"Who's the '*Schlimazel*' now, I ask you!?" hollers Schlimazel as he throws a stake whizzing towards his oppressor's heart. Then a *CRACK* of thunder and lightening! The stake hits an empty wall. She is gone!

"*You are!*" Her voice echoes from nowhere and she gives a little whistle—"Oh, *Igor! Boris! Ivan!*"

And from the shadows, emerge two hulking figures, Igor and Boris, local bullies from the village. Then a third man.

"Ivan?" remarks an incredulous Ludmilla to her recently jilted groom.

"Yes. It is *I!*" Ivan sneers to Schlimazel. "Also known as *Ivan the Terrible!*"

"Oh, yeah?" Schlimazel puffs himself up and bares his fangs menacingly.

Ivan has that look on his face just before he waxes particularly witty: "Boo! *Jew!*" And he raises his arms, *also* exposing a vicious set of fangs!

Hell immediately breaks loose. Boris and Igor, also well fanged, set upon Schlimazel and their battle quickly becomes a frenetic standoff, almost as if the strategy were to hold him at bay while Ivan goes after his former sweetheart.

The erstwhile newlyweds fly up and down walls the length of an alley. Ludmilla is now an adept fighter, but apparently, so is Ivan with his super-powered Cossack moves. And when she out-maneuvers him with clever *gong foo*, something always seems to fog her mind, giving the advantage back to him. They each wield the climactic wooden stake, but Ivan is the one getting closer to his goal.

Schlimazel has his hands full with Boris and Igor. In the distance come desperate cries: *"Schly! Schly!"* Schlimazel focuses and, finally, *THUD!* His stake thrusts deep into Igor's chest. Then, *THUD!* Boris gets staked as well. The big vampires fall to their knees, screaming in agony.

"Schly! Help!" calls Ludmilla. Ivan has her pinned and the two struggle over a stake pointed at her chest. Schlimazel tries to help but his writhing victims manage to grip his ankles even as their skin bubbles off horrifically.

"Hey Ivan! cries Schlimazel. "Sheep*shtooper*! *IVAN!*" Ivan looks up, just long enough for a speeding silver draydl to hit his eye!

"Yaaah!" Ivan clutches his bloody socket. He bolts from Ludmilla and runs off hollering: "You will pay, Jewish filth! And *you*, wench," he glares with one his good eye. "I will have you or kill you!"

"Shmen-derik!" shouts Ludmilla.

"Shmendrik." corrects Schlimazel, as he looks in disgust at Boris and Igor while they deteriorate into gooey messes, their hands now detached from the wrists but still clutching his ankles. Schlimazel and Ludmilla rush to each other's arms. Oy! They are too beaten and spent to give chase to Ivan. Or anyone else at the moment.

The bright moon illuminates the night. Not quite full, notices Schlimazel. One more day until the big one. He and Ludmilla had better plan and regroup.

———

At the outskirts of the village, fat Slobodan cowers in his bed, armed with a sword and a club. By the light of a candle, his zombified wife loads and then unloads an old, beat up linen closet—the one that the demon Schlimazel did not take. Slobodan imagines a noise and grips his weapons fearfully. It is only the wind, he realizes.

He was wrong. As two black clad figures burst in through his thatched roof. Slobodan screams and quickly trips over himself, almost breaking his neck. The intruders try to haul away the linen closet but the wife mindlessly clutches on to it.

"Will you let go, already!" barks Schlimazel's masked voice.

Ludmilla must sock the woman on the chin in order to get the furniture out of the house without a zombie attached to it.

And off into the hills scramble Schlimazel and Ludmilla, their new boudoir in tow, as far as they can possibly go before the sun rises. They are quite a distance from Sebreim when the first light appears and they wedge themselves into some dense forest vegetation. Once inside their cozy closet and out of danger's way, they are finally able to deliberate logically and methodically.

"*Oy! Oy! Oy! Oy!*" says Schlimazel, nursing his bruises.

"Did she really do that to your—you know what?"

"I don't want to talk about it."

"Why? Is now not a good time to talk?"

"Just forget about it. She's just an evil bitch."

"You like what she did, then?"

"I don't remember, for heaven's sake! The point is she's got half the village working for her! *That's* what you need worry about!"

"At least Ivan will not be working so good, now!"

"Mac Heath said silver can kill, maybe, if it reaches a vampire's brain."

"That *shmen-derik* has no brain."

"Shmendrik. *Shmendrik!*"

"Maybe we should just keep running. We could still make a life for ourselves, living at night as we are."

"*Oy!*" replies Schlimazel. "If the rat could hear us now!"

"Do you believe there is a Hell?"

"I don't know. We don't spell it out in the Jewish book."

"Well there *is!*"

"Then what would we gain by running away?"

"I don't know also. My head is too full of nothing to think."

"So is mine. Although I can't get the image of those rotting goons out of my mind."

"*Ewwwww!*" says Ludmilla. After a pause, "Are you hungry?"

"Starved," says Schlimazel. They both fall into a deep but restless sleep, tossing and turning with anxiety filled dreams.

Much later, Schlimazel stirs a bit. He feels like he is floating on waves. On bumpy waves. Very bumpy waves! His eyes open a bit. Something is moving. *They* are! "Ludmilla! Ludmilla!" She doesn't respond. "*Ludmilla!* Am I dreaming or are we moving?" Suddenly the closet *crashes* on its top, causing the inhabitants to crunch into their heads. Ludmilla has awakened with a start and tries to open the doors. Schlimazel restrains her tightly. It is obvious through tiny cracks that deadly sunlight awaits beyond.

"What is happening?" she gasps.

"I don't know. But it isn't good."

———

Outside, a group of clumsy zombies load the cabinet onto their backs again and continue on down the road. The muffled sounds of a panicky couple can be heard within the moving cabinet—an incessant blabbering of '*oys*' and a ridiculous but earnest young lady's attempt at Chassidic song.

CHAPTER 17

HOT TIME IN THE OLD TOWN TONIGHT

MANY HOURS LATER, SCHLIMAZEL AND LUDMILLA HUDDLE INSIDE their bumpy container. Light can still be discerned outside, but it is noticeably softer now. The box is suddenly dropped on its top again, causing the couple to crash up against their heads.

"What do we do now?" pleads Ludmilla.

"I'll always love you, no matter what," is all Schlimazel can say. But it is enough.

Suddenly, the doors are swung open and the box turned so that the two come spilling out. Into a bit of sunlight! It is almost sundown, yet the rays still burn with heat! They are weak, blinded and confused as a mob of burly zombies bundle each of them off in chains and dark curtains.

———

Shlimazel is carried somewhere then rolled out onto a large, soft bed. He has cooled down a bit and his vision is finally coming back into focus. The walls and architecture seem oddly familiar. Is he upstairs in the village inn? It is now dusk outside. And a very, big, bad, mean, ominous full moon is rising! *Oy!* He wears a ridiculously thick set of hand cuffs and wrist cuffs. *"Ludmilla!"* he cries.

"She cannot hear you," says the Countess, bruises gone and looking quite radiant. Schlimazel slips off the bed and stands up noisily in his chains. She playfully pushes him back on the bed. "We really need to talk, dear." Schlimazel, bound, weak and starved, cleverly decides that now is not the best time to fight.

"So talk," he says.

"Tell me what your problem is, sweetheart. That dirty peasant girl, still?"

"I will cut off the chase and tell you the exact situation," expounds Schlimazel. "First of all, she is the *only* one who I will ever love. *Forever and no matter what!* Period. End of discussion on that point. *Secondly,* I do not wish to remain in this state. It is an unholy lifestyle and to be honest, I would rather be dead! So you might as well give up on me, then."

"Those are pretty strong words, love. And more than a bit hypocritical, considering you just turned that little trollop into a bloodsucker."

"Oh, I had my reasons."

She laughs at that. "Oh, and I bet you did!"

"There is *always* a way out for the righteous!"

"You are so cute! All tied up and making silly excuses. Whatever is it that makes you so damned attractive?"

"They call me, *Schlimazel,*" he replies with a James Bond panache, unable to resist that one, even under the dire circumstances.

"Well *Schlimazdle,* my love—you don't mind if I call you *Schly,* do you?"

"No."

"Good—my sweet, sweet little Schly. My cute, darling, little vampire prince—"

"Get to the point."

"You make me warm inside for you. No, that doesn't describe it well enough. You make me *hot* inside for you! And just as I cannot resist you, *you* will not be able to resist me." And with that, she falls atop of Schlimazel, pinning him in a rather compromising position.

"Don't!"

"*Shush*," she purrs.

"Don't—" His strength is completely sapped. *Hers*, on the other hand, is immense. And her radiance and charisma are rising. Perhaps to the point of chipping away at his mind? *Oy!*

"You *do not* want to give up eternal life. And pleasures, incredible, indescribable pleasures. Beyond your wildest imagination." She moans and writhes against him.

"Just leave me alone." Schlimazel says.

"Just tell me what you want."

"And leave her alone, too."

"Will you be mine, then?" She is almost shaking with desire.

"Can I trust you?"

"Of course, my sweet," as she caresses her crimson lips against his neck.

"*Really* trust you?" His head is confused and resistance is waning.

"Of course, dear. Just lay back and enjoy my love." And Schlimazel, whose judgment in the area of trusting evil vampire predators may be rather clouded at the moment, nods his head weakly in ascent. The Countess literally groans with pleasure as she bites his neck, causing a delicious surge through his otherwise limp body. Her body is filled with passion and electricity. A passion that Schlimazel can somehow experience as well, as she sucks and sucks. Until he gets progressively weaker and whiter. Finally, she pulls her bloody lips away, panting with ecstasy. "Now you drink, my love, to make our bond *forever*." She scratches a thin red mark on her neck and offers herself to Shlimazl, whose lips are mumbling something unintelligible.

————

Meanwhile, in the village square, Ludmilla is chained to a stake inside the wicca man with dry tinder all around her. She and Ivan, who now has one eye, are having a pitched argument as pierced young zombie goths sit listlessly beating on primitive drums.

"Tell me before I light the fire!" screams Ivan. "The Jew forced you from me, yes?"

"No he didn't force me! How can you be so stupid?"

"I am *not* stupid!"

"Oh, Ivan, you are *so* stupid!"

"I am *not* stupid!"

"Why do you chain me here, then?"

"I don't know. Because—she told me so."

"She trains you like a dog because you have no brain!"

"She does not! I do what I do, because—because I—because—"

"See what I mean! Because of *what*, schmen-derik? Because of *what*?"

Had light bulbs been invented, one would just be flickering on in Ivan's head.

————

Back in the bedroom, the Countess holds her neck to Schlimazel's parched and aching lips. Just as it seems our dimwitted hero is about to succumb to an overpowering hunger and desire, she suddenly springs up to some cosmic alarm.

"*Damn!* I will be right back. Do not move!" She starts out, has a thought, whistles sharply, and Ludmilla's hulking mother and father shuffle in. "Keep him put!" she orders before dashing off.

Although he is far too weak to go anywhere anyway, the two fat, bedraggled and very soiled zombies sit on Schlimazel's knees and chest respectively. A moment later, Ludmilla's plump and filthy sister Peytunya joins in for good measure, setting her ample rear right on his face. Even in a semi-conscious state, Schlimazel mumbles in discomfort at this final indignity. Zombies, you see, have little control over their bodily functions.

———

In the village square, Ivan and Ludmilla continue their discourse:

"I want you for my wife. *Wait*—you *are* my wife!"

"Then take off my chains, idiot!"

"The chains?" says Ivan. "Oh yes, the chains, of course." And he starts to fiddle with her chains, trying to make sense of the lock with his one good eye.

"*Stop!*" It is the Countess, who seems to appear out of nowhere.

"Don't listen to that evil bitch!" yells Ludmilla.

"Yes, Mistress," says Ivan, bowing dutifully to the Countess.

"Stupid idiot!" adds Ludmilla

"Fetch me a torch!"

"Yes Mistress." And Ivan goes to fetch.

"What did I tell you?" adds Ludmilla.

"I will enjoy watching you burn," smiles the Countess.

"And when it comes your turn, you will burn in *Hell! For all Eternity!*"

"You will get there first, darling."

"I am going to Heaven!" Ludmilla says proudly.

"Not with *those* fangs you won't!" and the Countess breaks out laughing.

"Nooo!"

"And by the way, Schly is mine, *forever*. We just sealed it. His body felt *soo* good!"

"Noooo!"

———

Back at the Inn, three hefty zombies sit on Schlimazel, staring straight ahead, as zombies are wont to do. But if zombies could show any expression at all, Peytunya sure seems to have a surprised look on her face. And don't you know it, from under her plump bottom, where Schlimazel's head is buried, comes a reluctant blood-sucking noise. A healthy dose of color is creeping back into his limbs as well. Yes, desperate times require desperate measures.

"*Yaarrghh!*" gags Schlimazel, his strength returning. He manages to squirm out from under Ludmilla's family and scramble to the widow in his chains. He focuses his energy, does a quick Bruce Lee *hoop* and promptly dives through the glass. Again, if zombies could show expression, one might swear that Ludmilla's sister had a faint smirk on her lips.

Outside, Schlimazel crashes painfully on his head. Oh, well. Off he bounds, flipping head over heals in a manner that even chains do not inhibit.

———

In the village square, mindless zombified goth youths beat their drums at a rapid pace. Ludmilla strains in terror as Ivan approaches with a fiery torch.

"*Au revoire*, darling," sneers the Countess. And as Ivan reaches out to light his erstwhile Mrs., a yarmulked ninja sails down like a rock, headfirst, and soundly brains him. The dazed Schlimazel quickly scrambles to cast the torch away.

"Galileo would be quite impressed," notes the Countess.

"You lied to me!" shouts Schlimazel, holding his head and looking around nervously.

"Run Schly!" pleads Ludmilla. "Leave me in God's hands!"

"All's fair in love and war," says the Countess as Ivan lunges at Schlimazel. "And no matter how it happens, the night shall ultimately be mine!"

Schlimazel nimbly rolls aside, shackles and all, as the two rivals square off, circling cautiously as the zombie goths somehow beat a more syncopated drum rhythm—which Schlimazel seems to incorporate into little feints and parries. Ivan charges, but Schlimazel, his legs bound less than a yard apart, manages clever handstand turns, cartwheels and devastating heel kicks.

As a matter of fact, though not to Schlimazel's knowledge, across the earth, in the Portuguese colony called *Brasil*, a group of poor souls, oppressed and taken from Africa in similar maneuver-constricting leg irons, are developing the very same martial arts form, disguising it as a dance called *capoeira*[1].

But here, in a dirty little village of Sebriem, it is truly a sight to see vampires dancing the *capoeira*, next to a giant wicca man, under the surreal glare of a full moon. *CRACK!* Schlimazel's heel swings down into Ivan's temple with a force sufficient to kill a normal human.

"Break his skull!" shouts Ludmilla.

"You'll be toast *regardless* who prevails," reminds the Countess, who may be psychically swaying the fight one way and then the other, as Ivan lands a series of blows.

"Schly will never betray me!"

"He just did, darling. In your own bedroom."

"No I did not!" stammers Schlimazel, as Ivan hits him in the mouth five times.

"See!" says Ludmilla.

"OK, then. I have a woman-to-woman question."

"I am forced to listening." responds Ludmilla, all tied up. "Is this violence really necessary? Can't we all just get along?"

"What are you talking about?"

"Just go back to Ivan! *Voila!* He *is* your married husband, after all. He makes a splendid vampire and his father is quite well off, which never hurts, particularly to a girl from your position. It would really solve everyone's problem!"

"Yes!" shouts Ivan. "I would even spare the Jew!"

"Spare yourself, sheep-boy!" Schlimazel cartwheels a pair of jaw shattering heel kicks.

"Ivan will *never* have me!" cries Ludmilla.

"And she will never have me!" cries Schlimazel.

"Never say never," responds the Countess, her smile turning to ice. Suddenly the zombie drummers become a clattering cacophony, causing Schlimazel to lose his rhythm. Ivan quickly takes the upper hand. The Countess beams deeper on Schlimazel , clouding his mind.

"Do not let her influence you!" warns Ludmilla.

"*My* influence isn't the problem!" counters the Countess. "It's *your* influence that has upset the natural order of things!"

"There is nothing *natural* about your order of things!" sputters Schlimazel, as he receives a staccato series of blows to his face. And that's before Ivan shifts into some really serious damage. The Countess keeps beaming away as Ivan kicks and throws Schlimazel all over the village square, until leaving him semi-conscious in a heap.

"Last chance, darling," the Countess says to Ludmilla.

"Yes, be my wife! " says Ivan, as he goes to fetch another torch.

"I will have the fire first!"

"You're a dimwit, I tell you, if you think they'll take vampires into heaven!" snarls the Countess.

"You make me do this, Ludmilla! *You make me do this!*" Ivan arrives with the torch.

Ludmilla screams at him, *"Ivan, watch behind you!"* He stupidly turns to see Schlimazel spinning in a blur and hurling a whizzing silver *draydl*, like a bullet—right into his other eye!

"Yaaaahhh!" screams Ivan, dropping the torch.

"So stupid!" says Ludmilla. *"Soo* stupid!"

"We will see who is stupid!" notes the Countess, as the fallen torch ignites the tinder.

"Help!" cries Ludmilla. Schlimazel scrambles over and tries to disperse the flames but too much tinder has caught fire. And as if the situation isn't complicated enough, most of the village seems to be pouring into the square. Zombies armed with clubs, knives and axes.

"She should have settled for Ivan," says the Countess.

"You should have settled for Ivan and left *us* alone!" snaps Schlimazel as he struggles with Ludmilla's chains.

"I had though of it, but he doesn't have that *special something.*"

"Aaayy! I am blind! What will I do now?"

"They're all the same in the dark, Ivan!" calls Schlimazel as he vainly tries to smash a lock.

"Not funny!" says the Countess.

"No, that is not funny!" adds Ludmilla, in spite of the growing heat. Schlimazel makes a desperate foray into the throng of zombies and returns with an ax. *WACK!* He breaks Ludmilla's chains and *WHOOSH!* The two ascend out of the rising flames and settle on a nearby roof. Ludmilla grabs the ax and severs his chains as well.

Just as another group rushes into the square. This time, large thugs with large curved swords. And *fangs!* "I shall have him—or *no one will!*" shouts the Countess.

Our heroes assess the enemy below. The wily Countess, flanked by a team of sword wielding vampires, surrounded by a small army of hostile zombies. Run or fight, they ponder. "The way out, is the way through!" says Schlimazel, and he takes Ludmilla in a classic, Hollywood style, heroic kiss, warmly illuminated by a burning wicca man and beautifully accented by the light of the silvery full moon. A picture perfect moment if there ever was one, and not at all lost on the fuming Countess.

"Shall we, my dear?" he says.

"Why yes, my love."

"*Yaaaahhh!*" They cry out and dive, head first, into Death's very arms.

————

A climactic battle begins. And what a battle it is! Our heroes combat back-to-back with turning, rolling and flying team-work as they fight through a chaotic mess of thrashing bodies and weapons. Zombies must be heartily knocked out, but not killed, as the two are very conscious about saving their own souls. Fortunately the zombies often club or hack each other in the confusion, which isn't our heroes' fault. But the Vampires are another matter. Schlimazel and Ludmilla manage to wrest two swords each and have a feverish battle against the leaping, saber wielding bloodsuckers. Metal clashes and sparks, and the contestants fly all over the place. An assailant's arm is hacked off. A split second later Ludmilla rips a window sill and stakes him. A blood curdling scream. And another down for the count. *Oy!*

Schlimazel and Ludmilla seem to empower each other. They can feel the Countess's mind impinging, but True Love seems to have a force of it's own! And *THWOP!* A vampire's head is lopped off, which doesn't entirely stop him, but a stake soon does.

Zombies keep grabbing at the duo's ankles and they get dragged around until Schlimazel or Ludmilla can beat them off. At one point, they get separated in the pitch of battle. Ludmilla holds her own against several vampires as Schlimazel must fight one against four. Then a particularly bothersome zombie wraps itself firmly round his leg. And bites into his behind! *YOUCH!* It is Ludmilla's sister, Peytunya! Schlimazel is using every bit of his speed and strength to fight off a rain of swords and cannot deal with his leg problem. He can barely keep his head from being lopped off as he drags the plump girl around and around. And just before his buttock is completely bitten through, *CRACK! CRACK! CRACK!* Go a series of sickening head hits. The sister detaches from Schlimazel's aching rear and falls away.

"The little wench!" says Ludmilla, tossing a club aside and jumping into the fray. Our duo fight furiously over the next minutes, up and down dark alley ways until finally they hack, stake, hack and stake all of their opponents. Schlimazel and Ludmilla are left dazed and panting. After a pause, Ludmilla asks, "Where is the bitch?"

An armless opponent rushes them with a stake held in his teeth.

"Really now!" says Schlimazel, calmly removing the wood and thrusting deep in the cheeky fellow's chest.

"Yaaaaa!" screams the vampire.

"Let's go." says Schlimazel.

They straggle back towards the central village, where the sky is still bright from the burning wicca man. Schlimazel and Ludmilla are beaten and exhausted. It is getting quite late and the moon is looming lower and lower. Dawn may be soon approaching. *Oy!* And the Countess is nowhere to be seen. "This is bad," notes Schlimazel.

"Why must we do this by the full moon?" asks Ludmilla.

"That is what the rat said. He must know what he is talking about."

"Maybe we should separate and search." she suggests.

"That is probably what she wants, to separate us."

"What if we stay close enough to call each other?"

"Not a good idea," comments Schlimazel. But time is running out. And that is exactly what they do. Quickly and methodically they scour the town , careful to stay within a street apart.

By the outskirts of the village, Schlimazel spies the dark carriage, headed towards the woods. "Ludmilla! *Ludmilla!"* She doesn't respond. *"Damn!"* The carriage is getting further away and the first signs of dawn can be discerned on the horizon. *"Ludmilla!"* Schlimazel has no choice but to take off after the coach. He runs and leaps with all his strength. The carriage speeds up and manages to stay just ahead of him. Once they are a ways from the village, a door opens up. Schlimazel sprints like a bullet and finally jumps in. The door slams shut as the horses continue their gallop.

———

Meanwhile, in a dark alley, Ludmilla wrestles in the mud with a blinded, jilted zombie Ivan. They fight like cats over a sharp wooden stake. "I shall have you, or no one will!" screams Ivan.

"Exactly the words that *she* used!" shouts Ludmilla.

"I have my own mind in this!"

"Then let me go!"

"No! I *cannot* do that!"

"*See*, stupid!"

"I will show you who is *stupid!*"

———

On a lonely mountain road, the speeding coach shakes, shudders and bounces as some sort of mayhem goes on inside. The door opens and the Countess and Schlimazel spill out, holding each other's throats as they roll into the dirt.

"You scheming, lying bitch!"

"We do what we have to do!"

"But why *me*!?" And she flips him judo style and lands series of spinning side kicks.

"Because, I want your love."

Schlimazel adjusts his head to his neck. "A strange way to show it!"

"Who said life isn't strange?"

"Life is strange!" And Schlimazel breaks off a sharp branch. The two square off and do not say a word. The Countess looks at him in a way that Schlimazel hasn't seen before. For the first time—she seems vulnerable. "You asked for this!" says Schlimazel, ready to pounce. She just stares at him—and drops her hands limply to her sides.

"Kill me, then."

"What?"

"You heard me."

"I do not understand."

"Don't be a fool. *Do it!* Before I change my mind." Schlimazel hesitates, then dives on her. She falls willingly. He readies his stake. "Do it," she says softly.

But he can't. "Damn you!" he shouts, as tears are welling up in his eyes. "Damn you! Damn you!"

"If you won't kill me—then *kiss* me." A power of staggering proportion is clouding Schlimazel's mind like never before and he reels with indecision. She rolls atop him—and offers her throat to his lips. "Kiss me here." *Oy*—and he would be lying if he said he did not want it! "Take me now, love." And with a fingernail she opens a small wound on her neck.

"No," say his lips, but his eyes say something else. And from her white neck, a tiny droplet of crimson falls ever so slowly towards his yearning lips. Schlimazel's mouth parts slightly—but he jerks his head away *"No!* I can't. I *won't!"* She embraces him with a strength far greater than his own, and bites his neck with passion and fury. Her eyes light up with madness. Schlimazel is growing weaker and weaker.

Finally, she pulls back. "Now my love. Take me now. Take me forever and the world will be ours." She presses her neck hard against his lips, rubbing her blood wantonly into his teeth—and *THUD!*

Schlimazel drives his stake deep in her back! He spits out any blood in his mouth and crawls away, coughing and gagging. The Countess gasps horribly. She reaches vainly to remove the stake, but it is too late. *"Nooo!"* She screams. Her beautiful flesh begins to blister. *"Noo!"*

"I had to," says Schlimazel.

"I only wanted your love!" she cries, coughing up bile. "I only wanted your love." The Countess writhes in agony, her flesh bubbles and falls. "Please, don't look at me this way," she begs.

"This is bad..." says Schlimazel, turning away. "Oy, this is bad..."

In spite of everything, he can't help but feel some pity.

———

In the dirty little of village of Sebriem, just before dawn, mindless agitated zombies trudge around the embers of a burnt wicca man. Then a strange wind howls and passes, making them all shudder. And a peace comes over the village, as though a great weight had been lifted.

———

Down a muddy alley, sits Ludmilla, her eyes red from tears. Nearby lies all that remains of poor Ivan. A pile of goo and a bloody stake—mute testament to the results of a recent conflict. The sound of thundering hooves approaches. The fancy black coach pulls up and screeches to a halt. Out pops Schlimazel. "Like our new ride?" Ludmilla starts sobbing.

"He said he loved me when I pushed in the stake! I did not think I could be so cruel!"

"*Oy!* Darling! You should have heard what *she* said!"

---

1. Afro-Brazilian foot fighting, often done to music

CHAPTER 18

A LONG DAY'S JOURNEY
INTO THE NIGHT

THE HORIZON BEGINS TO WAX ORANGE WITH THE HASTENING dawn. But Schlimazel is so weak and dried out from his ordeal that Ludmilla must catch a wayward zombie to provide him a quick snack. Then, into the coach and off they go!

"Watch this," says Schlimazel, as they sit back in the plush upholstered seats. He pulls a lever and the shutters slam shut and dark velvet blinds roll down. "Not bad, huh?"

"Oh Shly!" Ludmilla cuddles into him. "Did we do the right thing?"

"I hope so. I didn't think she would be so pathetic in the end. It made me sick."

"You were true to me and killed the evil bitch. That is what counts." He strokes her hair and they curl up for the journey.

"The horses listen to my mind," he explains. "I will miss this once the rat changes us back."

Day breaks and the carriage races through the incredibly beautiful Transcarpathian countryside. Hills and lush meadows and then virgin forests with crystal mountain springs.

They make Romania by dusk. Schlimazel and Ludmilla

awaken to realize how filthy they are, but their wounds are mostly healed and they feel relieved that a great evil has been removed from their lives. If only they can remove the last of this evil from within themselves.

They must stop at a border checkpoint.

"Why would such a filthy Jew ride in such a rich carriage?" asks the guard. Ludmilla is upon him so fast that Schlimazel hasn't time to deliver the clever response he was preparing. The other guard has dropped his weapon and runs as fast as he can. Schlimazel chases him down for quick snack as well.

Then back into the carriage and off to Shlo-Liem Temple. The horses make good speed and hopefully this will be the last of such feedings. Although, to be honest, the two are enjoying it more and more. Blood not only nourishes them, it seems to fulfill and exhilarate like nothing else. They sit back ecstatically.

Ludmilla finds various compartments with items needed for a journey. Including soap, water and towels. And clothes! For her, at least. The two clean themselves and she changes into a dazzling new outfit. Ludmilla seems almost giddy as she applies some crimson lipstick for a final touch. She was always a pretty girl. Now she seems profoundly beautiful. And elegant, notices Schlimazel. Ludmilla smiles and laughs with a new abandon. He looks at her and has a scary thought for moment, but then dismisses it.

———

The night passes uneventfully and then the day. On and on through winding roads and trails barely wide enough for the carriage. Schlimazel falls into a restless sleep.

He dreams of the battle and hacked off limbs. Grotesque zombies and rabid vampires in a surreally twisted version of what had just occurred—and what had just occurred was pretty twisted to begin with! And then he dreams of the Countess. Laughing, beautiful and radiant. They roll and kiss and embrace. And she ever so delicately bites his neck. Schlimazel's body swells with ecstasy. Oh, this feels so good! And then, of course, he shudders with a large wave of Jewish guilt. And awakens with a start!

The coach is still. Ludmilla's face rests against his neck, staring up at him dreamily. Schlimazel gasps and pulls away. He feels his throat. Two small marks! "What are you doing!?"

"Nothing," she says.

"Don't tell me *nothing*! Why do I have these marks on my neck!?"

Ludmilla chuckles and then stops herself. "I only wanted a taste.

I did not take after that." And then in a seductive but entirely different vocal timbre—"*darling*." A tone too much like the Countess! Schlimazel grabs her by the shoulders and shakes furiously .

"Don't you *ever* joke like that! *Ever!* Do you hear me!?"

"Yes, I hear you. I did not think what I was saying." Schlimazel let's her go. The carriage hasn't moved since he has awoken.

"Why are we stopped?"

"The horses needed to rest and eat. We were killing them." Schlimazel looks outside the carriage. The horses are gone! He pulls Ludmilla out.

"So where are they?"

"They were eating by the grass over there."

"And you let them go!?" She nods, seeming bewildered. He is livid and takes off shouting and whistling for the horses. They are nowhere to be found.

Schlimazel crouches against the rugged hillside, holding his temples, concentrating, concentrating—on *horses*—focusing, focusing, focusing—until a nasty rock falls on his head. Followed by another. Ludmilla approaches. "You were going to change my luck, huh?" She chuckles strangely.

"You think that is funny?" Schlimazel asks.

"No." She seems startled at herself, then blurts out in a different but familiar voice—"*Darling!*" This not only scares the hell out of Schlimazel, it scares the hell out of Ludmilla as well. For something terrible has just occurred to both of them. "Oh my God, Shly! Do you think she is trying to get inside me?" And then Ludmilla blurts out another laugh— *just like the Countess!* They look at each other.

"*Yaaahhh!*" Schlimazel and Ludmilla take hands and run screaming into the night.

———

They run and scream like mad for many miles. Then they just run like mad, screaming only occasionally. Schlimazel and Ludmilla are making almost as good time as with horses and carriage, although this mode of travel, with its inherent trips, falls and stumbles is certainly less pleasant.

Not to mention the periodic crashes into a tree.

And then the rain.

And Ludmilla's periodic *Countess* fits.

"*Oh, darling! Take me now!*" Ludmilla trips Schlimazel and attempts to mount him. He tries to shake some sense into her.

"Who is inside in there? Tell me who you are!"

"*The Countess!*"

Schlimazel slaps her face. "Tell me who you are!"

"Ludmilla!" Slap!

"Tell me who you are!"

"The Countess!" Slap!

"Ludmilla!" Slap!

"The Countess!" Slap!

"Ludmilla!" Slap!

"My sister!" Slap!

"I was joking!" says Ludmilla in the Countess's voice. Schlimazel gives her a rapid series of palm and backhand slaps to both cheeks in a manner later perfected by Moe Howard. "Oh my God!" Ludmilla cries finally, in her own voice and breaks into tears. Schlimazel kisses the tears away and they take a deep breath before running and screaming again, off into the night.

––––––

The two manage an impressive distance until Shlo-Liem Temple is in tantalizing reach, maybe another thirty minutes. But the sun will rise in less than five. They must seek refuge and hurry into a small cave.

A moment later the sound of a furious battle emanates from within. Then a large scruffy bear scampers out, yelping. Our heroes mean business!

Schlimazel and Ludmilla huddle in the darkness, bruised and filthy once again. And fearful of things worse than bears.

"Maybe we should try and stay awake," he says.

"That is what I was I was thinking."

"Oy!" he says.

"Oy!" she adds.

"Not bad," comments Schlimazel, admiring her Yiddish. And the two do a good job of staying awake. Until they fall asleep.

A pain in Schlimazel's ass awakens him. *"Ow! Stop it! Ow!"*

Ludmilla is clamped onto his rear, sucking away. Schlimazel pries her off. She smiles sanguinely. "Have you gone totally crazy!?"

"No," she says calmly. *"Darling."*

"Who are you at this moment!?" demands Schlimazel, rubbing his backside.

"Why I am *Ludmilla!*" says the Countess's voice, trying to sound like Ludmilla.

"Ludmilla you say?" Schlimazel is suspicious. "So tell me, then—who is it that taught the rat?"

She hestitates—"The *rat*?" Schlimazel is now very suspicious.

"I'll give you a hint. He has a famous cousin."

"A cousin?"

"Ha—you do not know from nothing! It is the Rebbe Israel Baal Shlo-Liem! Cousin of the famous Baal Shem Tov!" Schlimazel edges away from her. "And I know it is *you* in there, *Countess*! You cannot fool me!" Ludmilla laughs in the Countess's voice.

"What a clever boy you are."

"Where is Ludmilla!?"

"It doesn't matter. I am back and that is what counts."

"But I killed you!"

"I didn't think you would go through with it, to be honest. Perhaps you will find me more attractive now, in my young, new body." She runs her hands over her thighs, tummy and breasts. "There is always something wickedly sensual about taking over a new body."

"Don't touch her!" screams Schlimazel. "Leave her alone! Or I'll kill you—*again*!"

"I'd like to see you figure that one out!" A good point. And then the possessed Ludmilla advances on Schlimazel. He backs away. She starts to spin in graceful side-kicks, causing him to dodge and parry. More spins and sweeps. More jumps and dodges. They are doing a dance of sorts. Then she flies across the cave and pins him, in a compromising position. He is still weak, due to his recent loss of blood. And she is quite strong, having just drunk it.

"So that's how it is. You go from body to body?"

"This is only number three, darling."

"Then who am I really dealing with? *Before* you were the Countess."

She writhes closer, insinuating her leg between his. Her mouth brushes teasingly against Schlimazel's. And in her sexiest, most seductive voice, she whispers, ever so softly—

"The Count."

This takes a second to sink in, then—*"Yaaahhh!"* Schlimazel has had enough issues to deal with already! Energized by this latest revelation, he weasels out in rapid motion and tries to escape. She pounces on him like a cat and they fight and scrap and fly around the cave and wrestle. "Why *me*, for God's sake!? Just leave me alone already!"

And Ludmilla/Countess/Count captures him once again, as though this were just more foreplay. Which it is. And she pins him down lewdly, holding his arms back as she runs her tongue up and down his neck. "No, don't, please, stop, don't!" Schlimazel is *really* not in the mood.

"I told you it was forever, darling." And she licks his neck. And then bites it. And sucks and sucks. Moaning. Panting. Her body undulating with pleasure.

Schlimazel is moaning too. Hopefully in pain, though, for his soul's sake, of course. Finally, the Countess/Ludmilla, whatever, pulls back, her fangs dripping with blood and her power and charisma at its peak. Then she forces her neck upon Schlimazel's teeth, rubbing her flesh until blood is flowing freely.

"No," says Schlimazel weakly, all dried out, trying desperately to resist the crimson nectar. It is futile, however, as his own lips reflexively start to betray him. This is bad! Really bad, as Schlimazel and Ludmilla seem to have *finally* lost all control of themselves.

And then, in the distance, comes a strange flapping sound. Flapping wings. *Bat* wings! A large *bat*, flying into the cave! With something on it's back. A *rat*! A bat with rat flying on its back! It is Mac Heath! To the rescue!

The bat lands right on Ludmilla's head and immediately tangles itself in her hair. She has a minor fit and tries to remove it, but Mac Heath throws some liquid on her face. A burning liquid. Holy water! From a tiny vial with a cross on it. Ludmilla screams and rolls aside, coughing smoke and gagging, but sounding more like *herself*, thank goodness. Schlimazel, dazed and weak, manages to sit up on one elbow, barely believing his eyes. "How did you teach a bat to fly like that?"

"If they can teach a rat to talk, teaching a bat to carry is not so difficult."

CHAPTER 19
BACK TO SQUARE ONE FOR PART TWO

AN HOUR LATER, AT SHLO-LIEM TEMPLE, LUDMILLA SITS IN A comfortable chair—with many chains around her. Schlimazel sits across from her, holding a normal sized vial of holy water.

"Your mother sucks wienerschnitzel in hell!" she curses in a demonic voice. He gives her a splash, causing a bit of smoke and grief. She stops sputtering and settles down. "Thank you," says Ludmilla in her normal voice, "I needed that."

Mac Heath passes by. "Not so much water, lad. Father Dimitri, from the monastery, was kind enough to offer that to me and we don't want to run out."

"How much longer?" asks the weary Schlimazel. "We cannot take this forever."

"I am going as fast as I can, as if things weren't compli-cated enough! An exorcism combined with a double, inter-faith vampire reversal! And that means *Latin* as well as Hebrew, mind you."

"I know some Latin," volunteers Ludmilla.

"You leave that to me, *mein* little Ludles. You will have more than linguistics to worry about when the fateful hour is at hand."

"Are you sure this is going to work?" queries Schlimazel. "No one figured on the damned Countess coming back—who might really be some Count!"

"I was meant to be a woman, damn you!"

Shlimazl gives her a splash, causing Ludmilla to hiss a bit, then shut up.

"Oy!" Says Mac Heath. "I could really use the help of Father Dimitri with this one, but we haven't time now. Every second the disease takes further hold, if we haven't lost your souls already. It was only a stroke of luck that I spied you through the telescope, going into the cave.

"That *was* a stroke of luck," reasons Schlimazel, not used to having luck.

"Your mother sucks gentiles in Bucharest and so does your brother!" Schlimazel sighs at his *luck* and gives Ludmilla another healthy splash of holy water.

"Easy does it!" counsels Mac Heath. "Now continue with both your sin confessing as soon as she comes back. I cannot emphasize the importance of a clean conscience. *Everything* will hinge on that!" And he scurries off.

———

"And when my sister's big feet stretched and ruined my shoes, I poured sour milk on her head." Ludmilla confesses.

"When my brother told on me for reading at work, I hid dung in his bedding." says Shlimazel.

"I sometimes would wear my loosest fitting blouse to the tavern. When I stooped to serve the ale, the sight of my large young bosoms dangling would drive the farmers crazy.

"Well it certainly drove *me* crazy every time you picked up a pencil!"

"And just *how* crazy?" she smiles coyly.

"You don't want to know how crazy!"

"I do want to know."

"*So* crazy, that I cannot tell you. And leave it at that!"

"*Schly*! Hello! What did the rat instruct us?"

"OK. OK. So I would go home crazy, from your lesson and —no I cannot tell you!"

"Schly! For the sake of your eternal soul! How crazy?"

"OK, OK. When it was dark and my brother was asleep—"

"Yes."

"I would, uh—"

"Yes."

"I would take cooking lard or some chicken fat, whatever, in my palm and touch myself in the manner of Onan—to cast my seed lewdly upon the ground!"

The sound of high-pitched rat snickering breaks out from across the room.

And the Countess/demon chimes in: "*Cooking lard, chicken fat, he didn't mix meat with dairy. But rubbed on a kosher wiener-- that,*

made him quite the fairy!" Schlimazel huffily splashes holy water on her face.

"Good!" says Mac Heath, trying his best not to snicker. "Keep it up, lad. Keep it up!" And he scurries off laughing.

"Very funny!" cries Schlimazel. "Very funny, indeed!"

"*Your mother strokes gentile wieners with cooking lard in hell!*"

"Yeah, yeah, yeah!" Splash.

———

Outside, an ominous storm brews. Lightening and thunder echo throughout the hills. On the steps of the temple, Mac Heath is laying out numerous scrolls and texts, weighted down from the wind by stones and illuminated by lanterns.

He looks at a timepiece, worriedly. Schlimazel carries Ludmilla out, still chained in her chair.

"Give her a dose of holy water, remove her from the chair and chain her to the pillar! *Quick!*"

"I'm hurrying!" says Schlimazel.

"No more water, please." pleads the real Ludmilla. "It is me now,

I assure you."

"Don't take chances," orders Mac Heath. Schlimazel does as the rat instructs. Ludmilla coughs and grimaces as Schlimazel chains her to the pillar. "Now chain yourself as well! Securely! The sun will be up shortly."

"Are you sure?"

"Do as I say! It is all, or *nothing*!" Intones the rat.

Schlimazel reluctantly secures himself to the pillar as well. "Are you *sure* this will work?"

"If ever you had faith, son, *now* is the time." This was not exactly the answer Schlimazel was hoping for. "Good!" says the rat. Now we begin!" His words are accentuated by an ominous round of lightening and thunder.

Mac Heath scratches his head, wondering where to start. He adjusts his little spectacles and scurries around a bit, finally settling on, both literally as well as figuratively, some Latin texts.

"*I will eat the flesh from your puny bones, rodent!*" curses Ludmilla.

"Sure you will, sweetheart, sure you will." And Mac Heath scrambles up a stool and throws some holy water in her face before delivering the first of a string of Latin prayers.

The Count, or Countess inside Ludmilla doesn't fare well with these incantations, as she struggles insanely with her bonds and vomits as though her guts were trying to escape.

"Oy!" says Schlimazel. "This is terrible! *Terrible!*"

With that the rat fires off an intense Hebrew incantation which makes Schlimazel's flesh crawl and start to blister.

"Yaaaahhh! No!" he screams. Until his own vomit chokes off his plaintive cries.

"We have only begun!" instructs the rat. Then another round of Latin and Hebrew. And more lightening and thunder! Schlimazel's eyes pop out and mucous runs profusely down his nose. He struggles to breathe and wheezes hoarsely.

Ludmilla struggles insanely to break her chains. *"Curse you, little rat! And curse the Jew beside me! I will survive you all! Curse you all to Hell!"* Punctuated by some projectile vomit and her head turning in a circle. Mac Heath throws more holy water and a really stinging Latin incantation which makes her eyes roll back in agony until she finally faints.

"Oy! Master! You are killing us!" pleads Schlimazel.

"If I cannot save you, better *death* than a life of destructive pleasure!"

"Easy for you to say!" And the heavens reply to Schlimazel with a lightening and thunder. Followed by a series of ancient Hebrew and Latin incantations from Mac Heath that fills the erstwhile vampires with such force as to make them shake like jelly. He looks at the two vibrating bodies and starts to think that this actually might be working.

"Oy!" says the rat, mustering his strength for the next round. For the stakes are rising rapidly as the dawn approaches. Schlimazel and Ludmilla start to feel the heat and perk to attention. "Ludmilla or Countess?" asks the rat, "or Count, whatever the case may be."

"It's me," groans Ludmilla weakly, sounding very much like herself.

"Good! Now hold on to your seats because here comes the hard part." The sun is ready to break.

"But what if we burn up!?" sputters Schlimazel.

"Then it means we cannot undo what has been done. And if that is the case, and you really wish to save your souls, then be prepared to lose the bodies that would otherwise betray you. But if your intentions are for the *greater good* and your *hearts are pure*, then maybe, just maybe, we shall succeed and you shall survive the ordeal!"

The sky brightens and the two are really beginning to bake.

"*Oy!*" says Schlimazel, looking at his sweetheart, his eyes filling with tears. "I love you, Ludmilla. I love so much! I love you no matter what happens to us!"

"And I love you, Schly!" Her own tears now spilling over. "I will love you forever! Even if I do not see you again until we meet in heaven!"

"*Love alters not with his brief hours and weeks, But bears it out even to the edge of doom. If this be error, and upon me proved, I never writ, nor no man ever loved.*" Recites the Shakespearean rat, Mac Heath, his own tears running profusely. And with that, the mighty Sun dawns upon the horizon and the Day breaks with all it's glory and portent. "May the Lord help you both!" And Mac Heath begins the final incantations.

———

Meanwhile, far away, but not too far away, depending where you are coming from, in the dirty little village of Sebreim, two armies are camped at the opposite ends of town. To the west, are the forces of the Hapsburgs and their Austro-Hungarian Empire. To the east, the Muscovites of Catherine the Great, Empress of Imperial Russia. And between them, bedraggled peasants, not quite zombified, but bewildered none-the-less, shuffle anxiously around their devastated streets.

The commanders and generals have decided to meet at the

inn for a final attempt at diplomacy—and if not a settlement, then at least some breakfast.

Seated across from each other at a long table, the plump young innkeeper's daughter pours them coffee. And the world-weary soldiers cannot help but notice how the not-so-coy little wench manages to display her pubescent bosom with a grungy-toothed smile at every cup.

"The peasants in this town are truly disgusting," says the leader of the Hapsburgs.

"I cannot believe we would fight over such a shit-hole," says his Russian counterpart.

———

After stale bread and some not so bad jams, it is decided to raze the village and fight another day. Poland had a serf shortage at the time and the peasants could relocate there.

CHAPTER 20

AND ON A PLEASANT WINTER'S DAY

SEVERAL YEARS LATER. IN THE MIDDLE OF THE OCEAN. AN English vessel cuts its way west into the brilliant setting sun. And far out upon the bow, stand a young couple. The fellow steadies his girl as she extends her arms and savors the golden afternoon's glow upon her sweet face. The moment is further enhanced by Irish immigrants on deck playing on their soulful flutes and fiddles.

"I feel like the King of the World," says Schlimazel.

"Oh, *Shly*, I never thought that life could be so wonderful," says Ludmilla.

"It was you who changed my luck, *Ludles*. It was you who changed my luck!"

The ship sails into an absolutely magnificent, picture-perfect sunset. And a starry night settles upon the placid blue sea. It is 1773 and radar would not have been invented for several centuries, so the blissful crew and passengers have no way of knowing what sharp and icy dangers might lurk beneath. But that is another story.

———

Three days later this ship makes port in Boston with its valuable shipment of tea. A cargo that Schlimazel and his Irish friends are employed to unload. *What a strange group of pale skinned Indians are assembling along the wharf,* thinks Schlimazel. But that is *also* another story.

This one ends here.

Acknowledgments

Thanks to my wonderful wife, Anastasia for her love and support as I scribble away long hours in my roof-top garret. More novels coming shortly, dear!

ABOUT THE AUTHOR

Richard Elfman grew up in the Crenshaw district of Los Angeles (made famous by the film Boyz n the Hood), was a semi-professional boxer, food and wine critic and successful stage director. He is also a noted Afro-Latin percussionist and with his brother, Danny Elfman, founded the band Oingo-Boingo.

Richard's theatrical career began in Europe, having worked with directors Jérôme Savary in Paris and Peter Brook in London. Elfman has been a published journalist for 30 years, focusing on food, wine and entertainment. He published culture and entertainment magazine and website, Buzzine, between 2010-2015 and produced 275 Buzzine red-carpet, music and celebrity videos.

Richard family include his mother, novelist Blossom "Clare Elfman", sister-in-law, actress Bridget Fonda, son, actor-producer Bodhi Elfman, daughter-in-law Jenna Elfman, niece, producer Mali Elfman and nephew, Emmy-winning broadcast journalist, Diego Santiago.

Richard resides in the Hollywood hills with his actress/dancer wife, Anastasia Elfman, where they are renown for their underground food/wine/performance salon,

"The Barbecue Bacchanals." Richard presently directs film as well as writes and directs live theatre and plays in the band Mambo Diabolico.

The Schlimazel of Sebreim is Richard's first novel.

www.ingramcontent.com/pod-product-compliance
Lightning Source LLC
Chambersburg PA
CBHW011153190726
48288CB00010B/3291